FOUNDERS' DAY FIASCO

FIREFLY JUNCTION COZY MYSTERY #13

LONDON LOVETT

WILD FOX PRESS

CHAPTER 1

*M*opey. It was one of those questionable words not actually recognized by spell check yet used persistently as if it had its own entry in the dictionary. It was fun to say, even if the meaning conveyed a lack of enthusiasm. It was the word moms used to describe their kids on the last week of summer vacation. It was the word often thrown in when someone was trying to recall the names of the seven dwarves but just couldn't remember the last one. And this morning, it was the most precise word this journalist could think of to describe the mood in her kitchen. In fact, if I thought about it, mopey described the mood of the entire last month. Even the dogs seemed listless as if they knew something was in the air.

Ursula was even too *mopey* to berate her brother, Henry, about the amount of eggs he'd piled on his plate. And Henry, who had cooked himself enough eggs to feed a small army, was only picking at the pile of yellow fluff. Both Rice siblings were too steeped in their dreary thoughts to notice that I'd emerged from the hallway. I took the moment of being invisible to glance across to the hearth, where, like the two people at the table, my resident

1

ghost sat with broad shoulders slumped and a long, stretched glower. He spotted me before the siblings.

"The nitwits aren't terribly entertaining this morning," he drawled.

I smiled briefly but was unable to answer. What I wanted badly to say was that he would miss them once they'd packed up their tools. I'd have to keep it to myself for now. It was something I'd become expert at, ignoring Edward and his droll comments when others were in the room. I'd been practicing the skill to prepare for the onslaught of guests I expected to eventually flow into the inn.

"Sunni"—Ursula had looked up from her cup of coffee—"I made a fresh pot."

"Thanks." I headed to the cupboard for a mug and poured myself some coffee.

"There are some eggs on the pan," Henry said. "I made them just the way you like, with plenty of butter."

Ursula scoffed. "That's the way *you* like them. Your heart is just one solid mass of butter." The fiery edge, the Ursula I'd grown to love, appeared for just a second, then she returned to her state of mopiness. Her thin shoulders rounded and she hunched over, her coffee cup clutched in her hands as if it might try and run away.

Ursula's clipboard sat next to her on the table. It was the infamous check-off sheet she kept of all the work that needed to be done on the inn, and it was the source of her sullen mood. In between all their bickering and arguing, Ursula and Henry Rice had transformed a once dilapidated, shabby Georgian manor into a shining jewel. Upstairs, the rooms gleamed in sage greens, pearl grays and soft corals. Glistening white trim and chunky, stylish molding lined the doors, windows and ceilings. Old rotted floorboards had been replaced, and modern light and plumbing fixtures had been installed to make the Cider Ridge guests comfortable. Of course, true comfort was still far off considering the lack of furniture. The rooms were beautiful but empty, along with my bank account. Restoring the inn had been wildly expensive, but in the back of my mind, I told myself it would pay off in the end when the Cider Ridge Inn was bursting with guests. However, that entire image of me running a bustling inn had become somewhat fuzzy in the last year. There were a few impediments to my plan, or at least one major one; namely, the brooding Englishman perched on the hearth with that handsome scowl only he could pull off well.

I filled a plate with eggs and sat down next to Ursula. She sniffled. Henry and I ignored it at first and pretended to be concentrating on our eggs. Naturally, being Ursula, she sniffled louder and longer. Ignoring was no longer an option.

"Here she goes again with the waterworks," Henry muttered. He dragged the fork absently through his eggs.

"Just because you have no emotions in that cold butter heart of yours." Ursula added in another sniffle for good measure. Her eyes were glassy as she smiled softly at me. "It's just that this place has been like our home for the last few years and you—" This time she pulled a tissue from one of the many pockets on her work overalls and blew her nose, loudly.

"Good lord, are there geese in the house?" Edward moved to the front window and stared out, his moment of levity cut short by his dreary mood. Edward and Ursula were both upset but for entirely different reasons. Ursula and Henry were finishing up the final room on the check list, the last bedroom at the end of the hallway and guest room number four. They'd be packing up their tools and moving on to other jobs. Ursula had been smartly posting photos of their work on the inn to their business website. They already had a waiting list. People with old, time-worn houses like the Cider Ridge Inn were clamoring for the Rice team.

"Ursula, we're like family now. You can come to the inn anytime. You just won't need to bring your tools."

The comment I'd hoped would help alleviate her misery, which was particularly acute this morning, only caused her to sob. Her bony shoulders shook. She used her tissue to cover her face.

"You could bring your tools," I suggested. "And they could just sit with us as we eat breakfast together."

Henry laughed but Ursula only looked more pinch-faced. "You'll be far too busy with the inn to visit with us, and you certainly don't need Henry eating his way through the food in the refrigerator when you'll have guests to feed."

"Nonsense, Henry can come over and raid the refrigerator anytime he likes." I winked at Henry.

"The man hovers in that ice box like a fly on manure and you're inviting him to return and continue to pillage and plunder your food supply?" Edward had pulled his gaze from the window to turn his focus on the conversation at the table.

Again, I had to ignore him, but that didn't stop him from continuing. "The only thing to look forward to when this place is overrun by chattering, giggling, whining guests is that these two fools will be irritating *another* homeowner. I doubt anyone else will put up with their nonsense like their current employer." He carried on about Ursula and Henry, but I knew better. He was going to be sorry to see them go.

Noisy and, yes, irritating as they could be, they unwittingly kept Edward company in a long, lonely existence where each day dragged into the next and there was no hope for an ending. He never failed to appear in the kitchen to witness firsthand their sibling carnival act, the Breakfast of Nitwits, as he'd so humor-ously named it.

Ursula wiped clumsily at her eyes. "Can't believe I'm getting so emotional. It's not like me."

Henry rolled his eyes. "Right, hardly ever," he muttered, then apparently decided a forkful of eggs would stop him from saying anything else he'd regret.

"The truth is, Henry and Ursula, I'd be hurt if the two of you didn't drop by now and then. It just won't be the same without you. Like I said, you're both family."

Edward scoffed. "From the nitwit side of the family tree, I suppose." Edward was extra ornery. He knew the final room was nearly finished. What he didn't know and what I hadn't voiced too much to anyone, I was having great misgivings about the entire Cider Ridge Inn idea. After years of envisioning a cozy, charming inn flowing with Emily's delicious food and the ambience only a century plus old manor could provide, the whole plan was starting to weigh down on my shoulders like blocks of cement. I'd be giving up my true calling, journalism, to embark on a career that I had literally no experience in. Owning a house that would make a spectacular inn was hardly a glowing resume for innkeeper. Five times out of six, I couldn't even pour myself a cup of coffee without spilling a few drops. And when I made my bed, it still looked as crumpled as it did back when I rushed the task as a teenager. Then there was the house itself. While it still lacked proper landscaping and bedroom furniture, it was the quintessential bed and breakfast in every way except one, and it was a biggie. Even Jackson had reminded me at least once a week that this whole business endeavor was going to turn Edward's world even more inside out. Admittedly, my tall, incorporeal Englishman was my main concern too. In the back of my mind, I knew it was going to affect him greatly. I was also keenly aware of how difficult it would be to ignore him all day long. Just sitting in the kitchen with Edward and the Rice siblings, I'd wanted to respond to him several times but had to keep it to myself.

Edward and I had grown close, if that was possible with a ghost. We both looked forward to our lively chats in the evenings

5

or on weekends when no one else was around. Jackson and Edward had a far more contentious relationship, but the familial ties were hard to ignore. Deep down, they both seemed to like each other. Jackson wouldn't be so concerned about how the inn would affect Edward if he didn't have some fond feelings for his ancestor.

"Henry and I have about two weeks left." Ursula's sad tone popped me from my thoughts.

I smiled at both of them. "You two are miracle workers, really. You'll have so many clients; you won't be able to get to them all."

The turn in conversation helped brighten Ursula's mood. "We're already calendared out for a year, but if you need us to come back to the Cider Ridge, you just have to call and we'll move things around. We'll always have room for Sunni Taylor on our calendar." This time it was me who sniffled. We hugged.

"The two of you are going to get me going too." Henry's voice wavered. "This is no way to start a workday," he said stoically, "all blubbery and teary eyed." He stood from the table after barely touching his eggs. "I'm going upstairs before I have to pull out my handkerchief."

Edward scoffed. "This semi-barbarian cannot possibly own a handkerchief. Unless sleeves count as handkerchiefs these days. I've seen him use those plenty when a good wipe was warranted."

I suppressed a laugh, another skill I'd *almost* perfected. There were plenty of times when I had to explain my inexplicable burst of laughter away as nerves or remembering something funny I'd read.

Ursula hugged me once more. Then, without looking up at me, she grabbed her clipboard and scurried off behind her brother.

Edward had returned to his sullen expression as he peered out the window. When the light was just right and his image crisp as could be, I could even see his dark eyelashes as they shadowed his blue eyes. "They'll be gone, but they'll immediately be replaced by more, strangers even."

I sipped my coffee. "See, you're going to miss them too."

"Never, how does one possibly miss an itch that can't be scratched, a pebble in one's shoe, a—"

"Right, right, I get it." My phone buzzed. I walked over to the counter where I'd left it next to the coffee pot. It was a text from Myrna.

"Prudence has called an emergency staff meeting. I'm not sure what's up, but she looks upset. She didn't even bring any bakery goods so must be serious."

"I'm on my way," I texted back. "I'll leave you to your day, Mr. Beckett."

"Yes, where shall I start that day? On the hearth or on the front stoop?" As he mentioned the stoop, Newman sat up on his pillow. He instantly hopped to his feet to look for one of his many tennis balls. The dogs were going to be impacted by the inn as well. I couldn't very well have tennis balls all over the house while guests were roaming about. It was an accident waiting to happen. I tucked that away as yet another check in the negative column, and that column was growing each day.

CHAPTER 2

*M*yrna was just finishing up with a swipe of lipstick when I stepped into the news office. She snapped shut her compact mirror, pressed her lips together to smooth out the bright red lipstick and instantly waved me over to her desk. I grabbed my chair and slid over so we could chat behind her monitor for a smidgen of privacy. Even though the only other person in the newsroom was Parker, the editor, and he was busy scrolling through his phone and seemed to have no interest or concern about the emergency meeting. It took some doing but Parker had essentially severed himself from caring about the *Junction Times*, a newspaper he used to live, breathe and exist by. He came into the newsroom, did his job, half-heartedly at best, and went home at a decent hour to be with his family. He'd settled into the new, far less stressful position, and it had helped ease his mind about his health. Less responsibility and worries meant less aches and pains and perceived illness. He was even down to just a few squirts of nasal spray and two to three lozenges a day, and I hadn't heard him mention a doctor's appointment in months. Now, all the tension and pressure of running the paper rested on one pair of rounded shoulders. I glanced toward the office door. It was closed and the small flowery curtains Prudence had hung were drawn shut.

"Where's Dave?" I asked in a hushed tone. "Or did he not get the memo?" Not that it mattered since Dave Crockett, lead reporter and sister Lana's boyfriend, strolled into the newspaper office whenever he felt like it. Prudence put up with his cavalier attitude because she had somehow convinced herself he was a star reporter. Not that he'd written anything too newsworthy since he stole my lead reporter position, but Prue had talked herself into his being irreplaceable.

Myrna picked up her phone. "Still nothing back from Dave. I texted him the same time I texted you and Parker, but he rarely writes back."

I glanced longingly at the small table where Prue usually placed the delicious baked goods she brought for staff meetings. This morning, the breakfast and glum moods had made for a poor appetite. A fresh banana nut muffin would have come in handy.

I turned back to Myrna. "And you have no idea what this is about?" I stopped and took hold of her arm. "Do you think she's sold the paper?" We both peered across the room to Parker. His brows were furrowed as his wire rimmed reading glasses balanced at the tip of his bulbous nose. Something on his phone had his undivided attention.

"I think Parker would know if she sold the paper," Myrna whispered loudly.

"She didn't sell the paper. I would know if she had," Parker muttered back without looking up from his phone.

Myrna rolled her eyes. "He's been dabbling in the stock market. He stares at the app all day waiting to see the lines go up."

A grunt came from across the room as he put the phone

down hard. "Not today. Everything is in a slump." He leaned back and crossed his arms over his round tummy. His chair creaked beneath him.

"Do you have any idea what this is about?" I asked.

"Not a clue. Probably some silly scandal with the snooty women's society or the nosy old crow charity trust or one of those organizations she runs. Maybe she wants you to do a new story. What did she have you on this week?" he asked wryly. "That's right. The annual pet show. How are the bunnies and guinea pigs this year?"

I ignored his barb and returned my attention to Myrna. "Whatever it is, I think it's pretty gutsy of Dave not to even show up for it."

Right then, the office door flew open. A whiff of Prudence's lavender perfume was followed by the woman herself. The ruddiness of anger and stress was visible under her ivory colored foundation.

"Dave has resigned," she said without any lead up. Just those three words, said bluntly and harshly as if they were bitter in her mouth.

The three of us sat speechless for a moment, then I chuckled. "That's impossible. I saw him just this weekend at my sister's house. He didn't mention leaving."

Prudence rarely sat during our meetings, but it seemed this morning's news was just too difficult to stand for. She pulled out a chair and sat. "Apparently, the other paper, a much bigger one from somewhere on the west coast, made him an offer last night. It was all rather sudden."

Myrna looked at me with wide eyes. "Did Lana know about this?"

"If she did, she never mentioned a word to me. But how is that possible? He wouldn't just up and leave my sister, would he?"

I spoke aloud but it was probably a better thought for the inside of my head. At least Prudence thought so.

"That doesn't concern the newspaper. Now we're without a lead reporter. Dave was covering the Founders' Day Celebration." Prudence actually had the nerve to look around the room as if trying to decide which of her reporters might now cover the event. It was insulting. I was just about to let her know that she could find a second reporter while she was trying to replace the first when she finally looked my direction.

"I suppose we'll have to let the pet show go so you can take over the Founders' Day events. The parade is Friday, the local holiday, so you'll have some catching up to do." She was speaking sharply and clipped because she was still getting over the sting of Dave's abrupt, unforeseen resignation. Had he said good-bye to Lana? Why wouldn't Lana have warned me? Or did he break up with her just as rudely and abruptly as he cut off his job at the paper?

"I'll get right on it," I said. I wanted the meeting to end, not so I could get right on the silly Founders' Day story but because I was anxious to get over to Lana's house. She was in the middle of planning a large wedding reception. I had no idea what was going on. We'd all just sat down to a nice dinner in Lana's barn, one of the few weekends she had free. Dave certainly wasn't acting oddly. For that matter, neither was Lana. They were even a little embarrassingly flirty at the table.

"I'll let everyone get back to work. Parker, I'm going to need to see the advertisement layout for the next edition. I had a few last minute requests."

Parker groaned like he always did when Prue tossed in some last minute changes, which in layout terms meant the entire paper would have to be rearranged. At least there'd be some spare space where my usual column went because it seemed I was now filling in for the absent lead reporter. I needed to find out what was going on.

Prudence's heels loudly tapped the floor as she retreated back into her office. She shut the door with a snap as if she was mad at all of us. The three of us exchanged glances, then Parker released another groan and gathered up his materials for the meeting on the ad layout.

Myrna shook her head. "Never expected that. Did you?"

"Absolutely not." I pushed my chair back to my desk and pulled out my phone. I texted Lana. "What's going on?" I wrote cryptically. If Lana didn't know about Dave's new job across the country, I certainly didn't want to break the news to her through a text. But it seemed I wasn't going to need to. Her text came back.

"I just ate an entire package of Oreos—double stuff."

I texted back. "I'm on my way."

CHAPTER 3

The only thing that kept me from driving wildly through the streets of Firefly Junction was the knowledge that my sister Lana was pragmatic in all aspects of life, even romance. Even if she was hurting deeply, she would do it stoically and with little fanfare. The Oreo text was troubling. The last time my sister overdosed on cookies, she had just signed divorce papers. She was clearly upset, but I felt reasonably sure she'd weather this small storm without much drama.

I pulled into the driveway. Lana's truck was parked outside the barn. I hopped out of the jeep and hurried along the paved brick pathway to the party barn. Heavy metal music was blaring out of the open doors. Lana never listened to heavy metal, especially not loud heavy metal.

I cringed enough at the sound to admonish myself for being such an old fuddy duddy, but that didn't stop me from plugging my ears as I headed into the barn.

Two work tables were set up in the center, the area where the tables and chairs would be placed for the reception. A pile of silk sunflowers sat on one end of a table waiting to be hot-glued to a linen garland. There was no sign of the hot gluer.

"Lana?" My voice drifted off into the tall rafters and the heavy drumbeats of Iron Maiden. I walked in the direction of the open supply closet and found my unflappable older sister perched on a stack of wooden crates, the ones she used for rustic weddings. She'd glued several sunflowers to her shirt. Her normally neatly combed hair was pushed haphazardly back in a headband. (I couldn't remember the last time I saw my sister wearing a headband and would have laid down good money to bet against her even owning one.)

Her lids were droopy as if they were weighed down. I glanced at the cup in her hand.

"Are you drunk?" I asked.

She laughed. "I'm not sure. Can people get drunk on Oreos? I suppose my blood sugar might be soaring just a little bit, which is giving me the look of a drunk."

"After a whole pack of double stuff, I would say soaring is a good word."

"And here's the real kicker." Even her words were a little slurred. "There was no milk. Have you ever eaten a package of Oreos without so much as a drop of milk?" The music blaring from the speakers was making the entire barn vibrate. I walked over to the radio and turned it off.

"Hey, I was listening to that," Lana complained.

"No you weren't." I gave her my arm to take. "Let's go into the house. I'll make us some tea, and you can tell me all about it."

Lana took my arm and held it tightly. My older sister rarely leaned on me for anything. Growing up it was always the other way around. I wasn't going to lie. It was sort of nice being the solid post this time around.

"There's not much to tell, except I am officially through with all men. Didn't we have some old great aunt who joined a

14

convent? Maybe I should give her a call." She ran her hands over the pile of silky sunflowers as we walked past the table. "I could throw some really fun parties at the convent. I think they'd like me."

"Pretty sure convent parties aren't a thing, but if there's one person who could make them a thing, it's you. I don't think you need to do anything quite that drastic."

We reached the house. Lana's normally spotless front room was unusually messy with a bed quilt tossed haphazardly over the back of the sofa and a pillow on the floor. The empty Oreo package on the coffee table looked as if it had been ripped open by hungry hyenas. There were chocolate cookie crumbs every-where and two empty soda cans on their sides next to the ripped cellophane.

Lana looked at the mess and laughed weakly. "Guess I had quite the night."

I tugged her along toward the kitchen. "Why didn't you call me?"

I pulled out a dining chair and pointed for her to sit. She plopped down as if she had no muscles in her legs. "Wow, I really do feel as if I've just gulped down a bottle of vodka. Who knew Oreos could make your head spin?"

I pulled two bags of hibiscus tea from the canister and set the kettle on the stove. "I'm pretty sure they're not meant to be eaten by the dozens, and if you were washing them down with soda—"

"Did I? Oh yeah, that's because of the lack of milk. Here's a little life tip to keep for later—you can't dip a cookie into a soda can. I tried and the result was a lot of broken cookie crumbs and floaty things in my soda."

"I will avoid that scenario in the future." I opened the bread box. "Do you want some toast to absorb the—you know—cookie mush?"

"Think that only works with liquor. Tea is fine." She yanked

15

the headband off, and her hair fell in her eyes. She swiped it off her face. "I've got to hot glue two hundred sunflowers to garlands today and look at me—I can't even brush my hair right this morning." She put her elbows on the table and covered her face with her hands. It was so unusual seeing Lana in this kind of state that I barely recognized her.

I sat down across from her. "Exactly what happened? Did you have any idea? I know Prudence didn't. She was mad as a rabid dog this morning."

Lana lowered her hands. The red finger prints stayed on her forehead for a few seconds before fading. Her brown eyes were glassy from lack of sleep. "Glad I wasn't the only ignorant fool. I had no idea. He just called—" she paused. "And no, he doesn't get brownie points for actually making a call. I know some people break up by text. I almost think that would have been better. I could have learned to hate him that much faster. Apparently, it was an offer he couldn't turn down. Some paper in California." She chuckled dryly. "He told me I should go with him, but that was just his way of easing his own guilt. He knew I would never leave Firefly Junction."

"What did you say to him?"

"I told him I hope he gets a terrible sunburn and then falls into one of those big earthquake faults running through the state. I also told him I hoped he got a flat tire during traffic hour, which I hear is almost all day on the California freeways."

"Good. At least you sent him off with some food for thought. He's already losing out because he's never going to find anyone as amazing as you."

Lana laughed. "Were you working on that line on the way over?"

I shrugged. "Could be, but seriously, Lana, at the risk of sounding cliché, you were too good for him."

"That was definitely cliché, but good to hear nonetheless."

The kettle whistled. I hopped up to pour the water. I returned to the table with our tea cups. "You already look better." I'd predicted right. My resilient sister would not let this get her down. She had way too much else going on in her life.

"It's probably better this happened sooner rather than later. I never saw us as a permanent thing. But enough about him." She snapped her fingers. "There, he's gone. What about you?" she asked.

I dipped the tea bag up and down in the hot water. "Me? Jackson and I are fine."

"No, this isn't about Jackson. It's about the other obvious problem that you are working hard to pretend doesn't exist."

My eyes rounded and I stared at her over my tea cup. "What do you mean?" Did Lana know about Edward? How was that possible when she didn't even believe in ghosts?

"Look, you are avoiding talking about your future business. Every time Emily or I bring it up, you change the subject. The inn is almost finished—"

"Not really. There's still upstairs furniture. Can't have guests bringing sleeping bags and then there's the landscaping. I have big plans for the backyard." As I spoke, her right brow lifted higher and higher. I finally took a breath. "You're right. I'm avoiding talking about it because, to be honest, I'm not sure I'm cut out for running a bed and breakfast."

"You'd have plenty of help from Emily and me, and you were going to bring Myrna on board."

"Yes, and I don't want to let everyone down," I started but she shook her head.

"No, you can't think about that. This is your business. If you don't think it's the right fit for you, then that's all that matters. Besides, the rest of us already have jobs. You won't be leaving anyone stranded. I know I've heard Emily voice concerns that there was never going to be enough hours in the day for her to accomplish everything. I feel that way too. So when you make this enormous decision, do what's right for Sunni and don't give anyone else a thought."

I smiled at her. "I rushed over here to comfort and counsel my big sister, and, as is always the case, she ended up being the comforter. Thanks, Lana, I'll keep what you said in mind. And you're right. It's an enormous decision. Now, I've got to get to work. I was just handed the lead reporter's assignment."

Lana shook her head. "I should have known he was a weasel when he kept pestering you about ghosts at the inn. What was that about again? Flying oranges or something ridiculous like that?"

I laughed along with her. Dave had spent days trying to find out why oranges were flying around in the kitchen. The whole investigation was majorly stressful. I was just glad it ended with him writing a non-newsworthy and basically ignored piece about the ghost at the Cider Ridge Inn.

"You're right. He was a weasel." I got up to take my tea cup to the sink. "My only sisterly advice for the rest of the day is stay away from Oreos."

Lana pushed her arm against her stomach. "No need to worry about that. I might have eaten my last sandwich cookie ever."

CHAPTER 4

*D*ave had left nothing of note for the story he was purportedly working on. It seemed he was too busy doing interviews with his new editor to worry about his current assignment. I had nothing but a name, Silvia Franco, and an address, the supposed hub of all the Founders' Day events, which included the construction of the flower covered floats. I'd attended several of the parades, and while the floats and marching bands were nothing like the ones from the world famous Rose Parade, they were nothing to sneeze at. The floats were a big deal. Teams worked a year in advance on design and ordering supplies and fresh flowers for the big event. There was a competition for best float. It was considered a highly coveted award… at least for the float making teams. And that, aside from being well acquainted with treats served for the big day, including foot long hot dogs and macaroni and cheese on a stick, was the extent of my previous knowledge about the Founders' Day event.

I was feeling extra pressured to not only get the piece done in half the usual time but to do it well enough that Prudence would once again consider me for the lead reporter position. If she was abjectly against it, then that would quite possibly push me back toward the idea of running the inn. It was one thing working in your dream job (journalism was that for me) it was another working hard at that job and never really being appreciated.

The float building and activity hub was housed in a massive warehouse just past the fire station. At one point in time, it had held tires, but the owner had sold off his product and rented out the warehouse for events like Founders' Day. I'd done a human interest piece on the tire warehouse. The shutting down of the tire business had been somewhat of a calamity for Firefly Junction because at least a dozen people found themselves out of work. My article helped alert other businesses that there were people looking for work. It helped match up some of the laid off employees with new positions. Last I'd heard, two had moved out of the area altogether and the rest had found work in nearby towns.

I'd left a message for Sylvia Franco, Dave's contact for the event. A small sticky note next to her phone number was covered with Dave's scribbles. I was able to discern the words *Founders' Day project leader* from the chicken scratch. Sometimes it was hard to believe Dave had managed to land so many reporting jobs. He did everything so half-heartedly. Even his messy, hard to decipher notes showed a lack of enthusiasm for the job. It was also still hard to believe that he was gone and gone for good, apparently. I was just relieved that Lana was taking it all with her usual indomitable spirit. I assumed the cookie binge was only a momentary lapse in judgment. All things considered, it was not even too monumental of a lapse.

I parked in front of the warehouse. There were at least a dozen cars parked in the now crumbling asphalt parking lot. With the number of people streaming in and out of the building, I expected a great deal of activity inside. With any luck, Ms. Franco would have a few minutes to talk.

The nearly overwhelming scent of roses washed over me as I stepped into the vast building. Four large floats were being assembled, one in each corner of the warehouse. It seemed each float had a half dozen people scurrying around with crates of rose petals, seeds and an assortment of greenery.

A woman rushed past holding a bag of hot glue sticks.

"Excuse me." I stopped her in her rush to the corner where a massive bumble bee was being covered with brown seeds and yellow petals.

She had on a volunteer t-shirt. "Yes?"

"I'm looking for Sylvia Franco."

She stretched up to look over heads and piles of floral supplies. "She's over at her desk." She pointed to a large desk set up against the center back wall of the building. A woman, who looked to be about forty-something and was dressed in a fitted pantsuit that looked as if it had come off a designer's rack, was hunched over a computer typing away.

"The blue pantsuit?" I asked.

"That would be Sylvia. She makes the rest of us look like slobs," she laughed as she hurried away.

As I made my way across a floor littered with more flowers and stems than an actual garden, I paused to let a man in faded green coveralls push a rolling cart past. The cart was weighted down with metal folding chairs. The man nodded a thank you. His nametag said Benny. By the grease on his hands and coveralls, I assumed he was the mechanical expert for the floats. After all, the floats weren't going to literally float down the parade route without some kind of vehicle beneath their big, flowery skirts. From the load on his cart, I assumed he was also in charge of setting up seats for the VIPs at the parade.

The cart rolled slowly past, and I realized I'd lost sight of Sylvia Franco. Fortunately, her bright blue pantsuit made her easy to spot amongst the reds, pinks and yellows of the floats.

Sylvia was at the impressive dragon float in the far right corner. She was leaned over talking to a volunteer who was gluing white petals on the base of the float.

I hurried across, determined not to lose my target again. Before I reached the dragon, Sylvia had skirted around the back of the float. She was inspecting the flower work on the dragon's spiky tail as I reached her.

"Ms. Franco?" I asked.

Her hair was black, so black it was almost blue. It was cut in a stylish bob where the front was longer than the back. The vivid green of her eyes seemed to be coming from a pair of colored contacts.

"Yes?" she asked in a way that let me know she didn't have time for small talk.

I lifted the press pass that was hanging from a lanyard around my neck. "I'm with the *Junction Times*. I'm doing a story about the Founders' Day activities."

Her nose flared slightly, and she glanced at my pass skeptically. "I don't understand. I've already spoken with a man from the paper, a Mr. Crockett."

"Right, well, Mr. Crockett left town to work on another paper. I hate to take up your time again, but if you could spare a few—"

Her neon green gaze looked rudely past me, and her nostrils flared more. "Brandy, what on earth took you so long? I told you to hurry."

I glanced back to find a short, squat women moving as quickly as possible on small, thick legs toward the dragon. She was carrying a box filled with coffees. Even with lids on, some of the hot drinks were splashing over the edges of the cups.

"Brandy, look at the mess you're making. Honestly, couldn't you put those lids on properly before you left the coffee shop?"

Even after being berated in front of all the volunteers, Brandy still wore a smile. "Sorry, Sylvia, the shop was busy, and they only had one barista—"

Sylvia waved her hand. "Never mind. I don't have time to listen to you." Sylvia turned a snotty gaze my way. "This is a reporter from the *Junction Times*. Could you please give her a tour and brief her on all the activities. But hurry up. I've got a dozen things for you to do. The coffee run took up way too much time."

Brandy kept that smile and bit her lip as she pulled Sylvia's cup from the tray. She handed it to her with a cheery glow. "Just the way you like it."

Sylvia took the time out of her scowl to taste the coffee. The scowl intensified. Poor Brandy's smile dropped to a worried frown.

"It's cold, you fool. You took too long." She grunted. "Never mind just take care of this reporter please. Brandy is my assistant. She'll be able to answer all your questions." She turned back to Brandy, who was still stinging from being scolded about the coffee. "Don't mess this up," she added snappily before hurrying away.

Brandy flashed me a polite, forced smile. "She's just a little tense. We're getting closer to parade day, and there's still so much to be done. Let me pass out the rest of these coffees, and I'll give you a tour."

"That would be great."

CHAPTER 5

*B*randy and I toured the other floats. She filled me in on the details, like how many thousands of flowers get used and how many pounds of seeds and beans are ordered. Most of the teams were too busy working on floats to take time for a reporter. It was a huge, painstaking task to glue each petal and seed on by hand. A lot of the volunteers were wearing head-sets and listening to music. I couldn't blame them. As exciting as it was to be part of a big float in a parade, it was also incredibly tedious to glue five thousand black seeds into the multiple eyes of a bumble bee.

Brandy was a lively, friendly sort, and I was just as glad to have been passed off onto an assistant, especially after meeting Sylvia Franco. Some leeway could be given to the woman who had all this on her shoulders, but it was hardly an excuse for the rude way she treated Brandy and the news reporter. I wondered if she'd treated Dave the same cold way. For a brief second, I had the urge to text and ask him, then I remembered we were no longer on the same paper or the same social network, for that matter. Lana would consider his name mud after this, and I was right there with her.

"I suppose Sylvia has a lot on her plate. Is she solely in charge of the whole event, or are there other people running things behind the scenes?" I asked. It was my first question that was focused more on the project manager than the decorative floats.

Brandy's cheeks rounded. "The city council is supposed to be managing from behind the scenes and giving the green light on decisions, but since Sylvia works in the city planner's office, they pretty much trust her with everything." She laughed airily. "And she takes this job very seriously."

"Yes, I got that impression. How long have you been her assistant?"

Brandy laughed again. "It seems like forever. She sounds mean and grumpy, but I'm used to it. That's how she always is when things get stressful. You know who you should meet?" she chirped and waved to someone behind me. "Benny, Benny, let me intro-duce you to the reporter from *Junction Times*." Brandy returned her focus to me. "Benny does absolutely everything around here."

Benny, the man with the faded coveralls and rolling cart, reached us just as she finished.

"Isn't that right, Benny?" Brandy asked. "This place couldn't run without him. He's even going to drive the dragon float along the parade route."

Benny nodded shyly and wiped his hands on his coveralls before deciding they were still too greasy for a handshake. "Nice to meet you, Miss?"

"Miss Taylor. Sunni Taylor and it's nice to meet you too. That must be exciting—driving a float in the parade." This was what my journalism career had come to. Discussion of flowery floats and the daring individuals who drive them. Maybe running an inn wouldn't be so bad, I thought briefly.

Benny shrugged his shoulders. "It's like driving a box with a small hole carved out to see the road in front of you. Doesn't take too much talent, but I admit I like being asked." He nodded politely. "If you'll excuse me, there's a problem with one of the extension cords."

"That's Benny. He's so shy but he's such a hard worker. Sylvia runs him ragged, poor man. Some days I don't think he even stops for lunch." Brandy's face blanched as she again looked past my shoulder. "Oh, Sylvia must need me for something. She's heading this way." There was an almost scared, deer in a hunter's scope sort of look on her face. She'd talked breezily and facetiously about her boss, but it seemed she was genuinely scared of the woman.

"Brandy, there are some purchase orders to enter into the computer." Sylvia and her preternatural eye color favored me with a smile for the first time since we'd met. "I realized I have some time carved out for an interview. I assume you'll want some direct quotes from the actual project manager." She tilted her head slightly to tell Brandy to take off. Brandy was more than a little confused. From what I gathered, the vainglorious Sylvia wanted to make sure she received all the credit and accolades for a job well done. She wanted to be the centerpiece of the article. She must have realized passing the interview off to Brandy was going to rob her of those fifteen minutes of fame.

Before Brandy was rudely dismissed, Sylvia's phone rang. She put up a finger to let me know she'd only be a minute, then she turned and walked a few feet away to take the call. That left an awkward pause between Brandy and me.

"I guess she wanted to make sure you learned everything you needed for your article," Brandy said. Brandy knew exactly why Sylvia suddenly decided to do the interview herself. Women like Sylvia were unabashedly transparent.

"I've told you before, don't call me at work. Just figure it out for yourself," Sylvia barked into her phone. "I'm busy." She hung up and rejoined us.

"Oh my, who was that?" Brandy asked. It seemed like a logical question considering how well the two women knew each other and how much the call had upset Sylvia, only the cheery assistant instantly regretted asking it.

"That's none of your business," Sylvia snapped.

Brandy's round cheeks turned bright red. I felt incredibly uncomfortable having to witness her humiliation. Surely, there were a dozen more tactful ways to handle it, but Sylvia torpedoed straight to the one that would cause the most shame.

"Brandy," she continued harshly enough that we both flinched. "Those purchase orders aren't going to enter themselves. And double check every number. You made at least two mistakes last time." It seemed the full humiliation wasn't complete yet.

Brandy nodded politely to me still managing a sweet smile. I wouldn't have been able to work up the same if I'd been in her shoes. It was hard to understand why the poor woman would continue to work for Sylvia. Brandy walked away.

"Now," Sylvia said imperiously. "As you see, this is a huge, important event, and I'm in charge of the whole thing. I start planning it a year in advance. As soon as this one is finished, I'll get right back to planning next year's event. It takes a great deal of commitment and time. You may quote me on that," she said and then looked at the notebook in my hands. "Are you writing this down, or should I start again?"

"No, I've got it. A great deal of time and commitment. Who designs the floats? They're all so beautiful."

"Local artists submit designs, then the teams pick their favorite. Then each float is constructed out of chicken wire. Our dragon float is clearly this year's stand out piece."

"So you are a team member for a float? I understand there's a competition."

Sylvia smoothed her hair with her hands. "Yes, but there's not much competition this year." Something told me she wasn't going to be a gracious winner, or, for that matter, a gracious loser if the judging didn't go her way.

"Why don't I show you my work schedule so you can see just how much time and effort goes into this event." She didn't wait for me to respond before heading toward her desk. Unfortunately, I couldn't think of anything less inspiring than listening to her drone on about how much work she'd done for Founders' Day. There were many more people, volunteers, team leaders, to talk to in the warehouse. The sooner I broke free from this woman the better.

CHAPTER 6

J had a fun discussion with the giant bee float team, a group of avid gardeners who wanted to remind parade watchers of the importance of bees and pollinators in our everyday lives. It was certainly a lively float and the big fuzzy bee was a winner in my book. The team hoped so too. Winning the trophy was a big deal. It made sense considering how hard the teams worked on each float.

The northeast corner was base camp for a giant pony float. The horse had a long flowing pink mane and green and white striped tail. It reminded me of the My Little Pony toys I played with as a kid.

I hadn't noticed that Sylvia was standing at the pony float until I heard her cutting tone as she spoke harshly to a woman with short blonde hair and a frilly apron covering her overalls. It seemed the apron had been customized for the team since they all wore the brown checked aprons. A pony matching the float had been artistically drawn onto each apron.

"You're only trying to make things more difficult because you know we're going to win this year," the woman spoke back with just as harsh a tone. After watching her verbally abuse her assistant all morning, it was nice seeing someone stand up to Sylvia.

Sylvia's laugh (yes it bordered on a cackle) echoed off the tall ceiling. "Please, this looks like something a team of kindergartners whipped up. I should never have allowed it into the parade."

"Ours looks childish? With your stupid and unoriginal dragon you'll be the laughingstock of the event. Now, leave us alone, and go find someone else to harass, you witch."

Sylvia was taken aback by the witch comment. Her lips pulled in and out as if she was working on a proper retort but couldn't find the right words. Her complexion turned red. She lifted a finger and pointed rudely at the woman's face. The rest of the pony team had now stopped their work to watch the argument.

"Watch yourself, Christy. I can have you removed from the parade, and I'll send you the bill for the flowers you've wasted."

"You wouldn't dare," Christy said. I was mentally applauding the woman for standing her ground. Sylvia seemed to be a first class bully. A bully without much backbone. She sneered at Christy, turned on her heels and marched away. I stepped off to the side so as not to be run over during her retreat. She didn't even see me in her fit of anger. The journalist in me was thinking there was a better story here than just the building of floats for a parade. But the current owner of the *Junction Times* was not keen on controversy. Even though it sold copies, Prudence liked to keep scandal out of her paper.

I waited for the cloud of tension to clear from the air before I made my way to the pony float. I realized that I was almost lightheaded from the overwhelming scent of flowers filling all air space in the building. I assumed the workers were used to it.

Christy appeared to be close in age to her rival, Sylvia. On closer inspection, her perfectly shaped brows were mostly drawn in and her long lashes were fakes.

"Hello, I'm Sunni Taylor with the *Junction Times*." I flashed my press pass.

Christy straightened and smoothed her hand over her apron. "Oh, the *Junction Times*. I love that paper. And you're Sunni Taylor. I love your column, but I thought Dave Crockett was covering the event." She looked past me anxiously, apparently hoping to see Dave. "He's lead reporter, isn't he?" she asked. Just when she had me liking her even more, she fell down a few pegs by looking disappointed that her float was not going to be covered by the lead reporter. No wonder she and Sylvia were butting heads. They were two peas in a pod. The pristine overalls and folksy apron should have been a dead giveaway.

"Dave is no longer covering Founders' Day," I said and added a smile. "You're stuck with me."

"No problem. As you can see, we're hard at work on the pony. We thought it would be a nice treat for the kids watching the parade. We've named him Spunky after a pony my assistant, Marilyn, had as a little girl."

"He certainly looks Spunky." It almost made my teeth hurt thinking how cutesy and sweet this whole story would be, even though there was obvious tension behind the scenes. I decided to dig a little further into the good stuff, namely, the aforementioned tension. "As I walked up, it seemed that you and the project manager, Sylvia Franco, were having a disagreement."

Her heavy fake lashes fluttered nervously, then she added in an edgy laugh. "No, no, no disagreement. Sylvia just tends to take her position a little too seriously. We're all used to her bossiness. We just laugh it off."

I had definitely not seen any moment that could be described as 'laughing it off', but it seemed Christy wasn't going to give up the goods. On anything, for that matter.

She glanced around abruptly. "Marilyn, there you are." She waved to a woman with dark green cat eye shaped glasses. The woman looked up from her armful of greenery. "This nice reporter from the *Junction Times* has some questions to ask. Maybe you could show her our original designs and explain how the float gets built. I need to make some phone calls." Christy turned her fake smile back to me. "If you don't mind—Marilyn will take good care of you." Off she dashed. Yep, two peas in a pod, and I was being passed off to an assistant again. I wondered if Christy would also suddenly realize she was going to miss out on being mentioned in the newspaper and return to talk to me. I also wondered whether she would have stuck around if Dave Crockett had been conducting the interview. Either way, I was hoping the assistant would be more forthcoming about the argument I'd witnessed.

Marilyn seemed somewhat flabbergasted that she had to stop what she was doing and take over as tour guide, but just like Brandy, Christy's assistant approached me with a polite smile.

"I'm sorry to take you away from your work," I said. "We can make this quick." And I meant it. I saw the float and how it was being glued together, there wasn't much else to learn.

"No problem. Now, let me see where the design plans were placed. That's right. They're on the work table." I followed her, even though I wasn't the least bit interested in the design plans.

"I guess the competition between these floats is kind of a big deal," I noted.

A short laugh burst from her mouth. "You could say that. I mean, most of us are just here for the camaraderie. It's a lot of fun working on these floats, but some people, usually the team leaders, take it very seriously. It's just a silly, old trophy, but people act like they're winning a Nobel Prize."

We reached the work table. It was cluttered with glue sticks, empty coffee cups, scissors and various notes. The designs were under the debris. Marilyn had to do a little digging to get them free. The plans were professionally drawn by someone with architectural skills. They were far more detailed than I expected.

"When I walked over to your float, I happened upon an argument or what looked like an argument between Sylvia Franco and Christy."

A nervous little sound that was meant to be a laugh but came out too throaty followed. "That? That was just healthy competition." Marilyn looked around to see if we were alone, which, aside from the dozens of people scurrying around the building, we were. "Sylvia and Christy have a long history, so they're extra competitive, you know, like two siblings. Not that they're siblings, of course, because they're not. Not even sure if they're friends anymore." Marilyn pushed her fingers against her lips to physically stop the flow of words. "Oops. Not sure if that's public knowledge." Her entire face frowned. "You won't write that in the paper, will you? I'll never get to work here again, and I look forward to this float building every year."

I patted her arm. "I won't mention it. You said the two women have history?"

Her brown eyes darted around the room. It was clear she was looking out for Christy, but she hadn't returned from making phone calls. I could only assume Christy was waiting for me to clear the area before returning. "Not a history, exactly. Their kids go to the same schools. You know how those PTA moms are. I think they both ran for president of the PTA, and things got pretty heated." It seemed now that there was a crack in the dam, Marilyn was just going to let things flow. "It was like a nasty political fight, names were called, enemies made, but it was just good ole' rivalry."

"Who won?" I asked.

"Uh, one of the fathers, I think. Both Sylvia and Christy made such a mess of it, everyone decided to throw their vote toward the underdog. If there's anything you'd like to know about creating the float just ask. I've been doing this for years." It seemed she was done talking about the 'good ole rivalry' between Sylvia and Christy, and we were back to discussing floats. Here I was doing the lead story, and I might as well have been covering the pet show.

CHAPTER 7

Once I'd finally cleared the floral perfume from my head, my stomach kicked into lunch gear. After the long morning, I was looking forward to meeting Jackson for lunch at Layers. A Cary Grant, roast beef on sourdough with a side of coleslaw, seemed just what I needed. Jackson had gotten there first and put in our orders. He was picking up the food when I walked inside.

He motioned his head toward the dining area. "Grabbed our usual table by the window."

I followed him to the table and plopped down ready for a break.

Jackson's mouth tilted in a crooked grin. "That sounded as if you had a long morning."

I sat forward. "Oh my gosh, I haven't told you the big news. I was so heady with the scent of roses—"

"Did you say roses?" His brow arched dramatically. "Roses from who?"

I laughed. "Whoa there, Mr. Jealousy. Not that I mind you

being jealous, but I was at the warehouse where they're constructing floats for the parade."

His shoulders actually relaxed, which gave me just a little spark of joy.

"That is so cute," I teased.

"I wasn't jealous." He shrugged. Jackson was one of the few people who could pull off a confident shrug. "All right. I was jealous. So what was the big news?" He bit his pickle and chomped on it while he waited for me to tell him.

"Dave has left."

"Dave," he repeated, then his brows lifted. "You mean Dave. Lana's Dave."

"Yep, but not anymore."

"They broke up?" he asked with about the normal amount of enthusiasm you could expect from most men. Why weren't they ever more intrigued by relationship gossip? It was aggravating. Whenever something noteworthy was happening at the precinct, he only ever knew the most surface-y details, and it drove me nuts. Even things like what did Officer Nunes have, a girl or a boy? His go-to answer was 'yeah, one of those, just can't remember which'.

"You could say that Dave broke up with the whole thing, the *Junction Times*, the town, my sister. He's gone. West coast."

"No kidding. Did Lana know? Didn't we just see him this weekend? Does that mean you are lead reporter?" He was tossing in a few extra questions so he could get in some good bites on his sandwich.

"Not kidding. No, she didn't as evidenced by the now empty cookie package on her coffee table. Yes, we just saw him, but apparently, he was keeping it all secret. And no, I'm not lead reporter… yet. However, I did get handed Dave's assignment, which isn't much more interesting than the pet show." I picked up my sandwich. "I think that covers everything."

"You should be lead reporter. Why didn't she give you the job?"

"Because she thinks I'm leaving the paper soon to start the bed and breakfast." I ripped open a packet of sugar and poured it into my tea. "At least that was the reason she gave me when she hired Dave. Or maybe she just isn't that impressed with my skills. Not that she would know what good journalistic skills were even if they bit her in that big, round—" I took a bite to stop myself from finishing the sentence. Even unfinished, it gave Jackson a good laugh. He was not a fan of Prudence, solely based on my personal accounts of the woman and her leadership style. She had clearly played favorites, and now her golden boy had up and left without so much as a farewell. It was hard not to feel a little pleased by the way things turned out. (Except for the whole Lana thing. She didn't deserve it.)

Jackson was a world class sandwich eater. He had finished his Bela Lugosi and was eyeing the second half of my Cary Grant. The sandwiches were always just a smidgen too big for me. It seemed bakers should make a bread loaf that was somewhere between a baguette and a full loaf, something that would create just the right amount of sandwich. Lucky for Jackson, no baker had come up with that brilliant idea, so I handed him my second half. He always asked 'are you sure?' just before plowing it into his mouth, which I always found cute and a little annoying. Once, I said no suddenly as the sandwich had already entered his mouth. He froze and stared at me over it, afraid to clamp down his jaw and at the same time, reluctant to remove it from his teeth. I had a great laugh, but it didn't stop him from still asking just as he shoved the sandwich toward his mouth.

"So," Jackson started after downing half of the half. "You said 'she thinks'."

I stared at him over my pickle. "I'm not following."

He grinned into his napkin as he wiped his face. "You said

Prudence *thinks* you're going to leave the paper soon. Not that she knows you're leaving but that she thinks you're leaving."

"Did I say that?" I fidgeted with the napkin on my lap, my eyes diverted by the same napkin.

"Sunni? What's going on in that super smart brain of yours? I've been sensing that the closer the inn is to being finished, the further you get from the reality of opening it up. I noticed you were in no hurry to get furniture for the bedrooms."

"Yes, well that has more to do with my bank account and less to do with indecision—" I used the wrong word.

Jackson snapped his fingers. "I knew it. You're not decided about starting the bed and breakfast."

The vinyl upholstery on the booth squeaked as I rested against it. "You're right. I'm just not sure I want to give up my career. Not that it's anything to rave about right now. I mean, I'm covering a Founders' Day parade. Not exactly the intrigue and headline breaking news I'd dreamt of in college. Still, I love writing for the paper. And the inn—well—I'm just not sure it's for me. Lana and Emily had pushed the idea. At the time it sounded so fun. But I realized, my sisters are exactly the types to run a bed and breakfast. They're great at being hostesses and decorating and cooking and organizing. I could go on and you could stop me anytime because it is making my skills look embarrassingly shabby by comparison."

"Your skills are not shabby. How often has either Lana or Emily solved a murder? And you can run faster and climb trees higher than both your sisters, and most everyone, for that matter."

I leaned my head and took a long moment to admire him. "Now I'm glad I gave you my sandwich. But you see what I mean, don't you?"

Jackson nodded. "All I know is you can do anything you set your mind to, but if opening the inn doesn't feel right for you, then I think you should skip it or put it off for another time. Besides, I know a certain ghost who'll be more than happy not to have guests overrun his home."

I sat forward. "That is so sweet. See, you were worried about Edward. You kept mentioning the way it was going to affect him and make his existence much harder."

"I just think having him there is going to make it harder for you to run the inn smoothly. You know, with him hovering around like a vulture in a waistcoat. It's hard enough trying to ignore him when it's just your sisters or Raine in the kitchen. I can't even imagine how hard it would be with a bunch of strangers drifting in and out of the rooms."

I smiled at him for a long moment. "Come on, admit it. You were worried about him."

"Why would I worry about a ghost?" he asked a little too loudly, causing a few heads to turn our direction. "Oops. See, we're sitting in a restaurant, and he's still making our lives harder. He's like that big horse fly who zips into the barn and won't go away no matter how many times you swat at it."

"Speaking of barns and horses—if I did decide to just stay on at the paper and not open the inn, I was thinking of adding a barn and maybe a few animals. I know you've been dreaming about owning a horse."

His eyes lit up like a kid. "Seriously? That would be great." He tamped down his enthusiasm. "But I don't want that to be the deciding factor. You've been dreaming about this business since you moved here. Make sure you're doing it for you." He reached across, and I took his hand. "I'm behind you no matter what you decide."

"Thanks. It's good to have your support because I can tell you I've been spending a lot of time on this dilemma. And, I confess, Edward Beckett has been bouncing around in the mind debate just like he bounces Newman's balls off the walls. There's no way to ignore him. He might be transparent, but he's a huge presence and impossible to ignore. If you told me five years ago I'd be taking a ghost's feelings into consideration on a huge life decision, I would've told you you were bonkers. In fact, even hearing it now feels a little nuts."

Jackson lifted his glass for a toast. "Here's to both of us now being solidly bonkers."

CHAPTER 8

*E*mily had texted that Nick was away for two days on a golf trip and if I came to help with the animals she'd make me a triple grilled cheese sandwich with homemade pickles and fresh tomatoes. Considering my dinner prospects were whatever was left in the freezer, it was an offer I could not refuse. Not only that, I loved helping with the animals.

Emily was just rolling a wheelbarrow full of hay to the barn when I walked up. It was a lovely spring evening. The sun was just high enough to give us plenty of light and still cast beautiful pale gray shadows over the farm. Emily was wearing some khaki green overalls rolled up at the ankles and her brown work boots. I could easily imagine myself in the same outfit, pushing a wheelbarrow out to a barn to feed horses and goats. Maybe I'd have a few of those cute alpacas too. I hadn't really considered myself the farmer type until Emily and Nick started their wonderful farm. And when Jackson, one day, offhandedly, mentioned that he'd like to have a farm, the idea really started taking root. Every time I visited Emily, I tried to picture myself doing the chores, spending long days outside with animals and vegetable gardens and the earthy warm smells that went along with all of it, and the visions always pleased me.

"Don't dawdle," Emily called. "I need you to fill water buckets. Start with the goats. And don't spend too long cuddling them. Chores first, snuggles later." Emily was always extra cute when she tried to be bossy. It was hard to take a woman who looked like a cross between Cinderella and Cindy Lou of Whoville seriously, but I saluted to let her know I was going to follow orders. That was right after I gave each goat a quick cuddle.

Tinkerbell looked up first wondering if her dinner had arrived. *I* was disappointed that *she* seemed disappointed to find it was only me. But that didn't stop me from wrangling her into my arms and giving her a hearty squeeze. I did the same to Cuddlebug before picking up the water buckets. I headed out of the stall. Emily was standing at Butterscotch's stall heaving large flakes of hay inside.

"I asked Lana to join us, but she said she wasn't in the mood." Emily stopped her task and was wearing a great deal of the hay. She flicked a piece out of her hair. "I can't believe that Dave. What a stinker. I mean, not so much as a hint that he was even applying for a new job. I never liked him," she added. "Poor Lana. Do you think she'll be all right?"

I laughed. "We are talking about Lana Taylor, our big sister, right?"

Emily smiled and nodded. "You're right. What am I thinking? Of course she'll be all right. I do worry that she's not going to trust anyone after this."

Emily rolled the wheelbarrow to the goat stall. They both began a chorus of low, excited bleats. I tossed in the hay and made a point to let them know it was coming from Auntie Sunni, though they didn't seem to care about the source as much as I thought they would. Emily grabbed one of the water buckets, and we walked out of the barn and back into the dusky light.

Sunset was always extra beautiful at Emily's farm. We lived along the same stretch of land, but somehow, it always looked and felt more bucolic, more fairy tale-like at Emily's farm. It might have been the low cooing sounds of the chickens or the horse's soft snorts as she lazily grazed on her dinner or maybe it was because Emily and Nick had done such an amazing job turning their old farmhouse into the coziest, most welcoming place on earth. Could the Cider Ridge Inn ever feel as homey? Ursula and Henry had made it gleam like a house in a magazine. It was up to me to make it welcoming. Even if I never opened the door to guests, I wanted to have what Emily and Nick and even Lana had. A house that was always a marvelous place to come home to. After all the construction and remodeling, I hadn't had time to make the place my own. That would change once the tools and ladders were gone... no matter what I decided about the bed and breakfast.

Emily and I filled the buckets and carried them back to the barn. The chickens were already in for the night. Emily always put them in before dusk and let them out well after dawn to avoid what she liked to call 'those predatory beasts that lurk in the shadows'.

"Em, do you think I'd make a good farmer?"

The laugh that spurted from her mouth did not boost my confidence on the matter. Then her blue eyes sparkled my direction. "Oh, you're serious?"

"Well, as I recall, you grew up in the same suburban house and neighborhood as me, and you managed a transition to farm life just fine. It's not as if I'm Ava Gabor on Green Acres. I do like to get my hands dirty, and I love the outdoors and the animals."

I sensed that Emily was feeling bad for laughing. At the same time, she seemed to still be wondering if I was being serious or if I was about to spring a *gotcha* on her.

"But what about the inn?" she asked, and rightfully so.

We paused our conversation to place the water buckets in stalls. I used the interim to organize my response. There weren't too many ways to do that, so I just blurted it out as we stood in the barn aisle with the soft, *snuffly* sounds of animals eating and the warm, musky scent that came with those same animals.

"I'm not sure I want to open the inn." My words hung in the damp air for a moment as we looked at each other, two sisters who knew each other better than we knew ourselves.

"I knew that," she said. "I was just waiting for you to say it. Let's go to the house and make grilled cheese, then we can talk about it."

Emily sawed off thick slices of her homemade sourdough bread while I grated a mound of sharp white cheddar. Emily insisted that grilled cheese sandwiches were better when made with grated cheese. Who was I to argue?

"How long have you known?" I finally asked after we'd finish discussing the all important topic of the follow-up dessert. Emily always had homemade ice cream in her freezer. She experimented with a lot of flavors before finding the perfect one to post about on her blog. At the moment, caramel and butter pecan was nestled in the freezer just waiting for a good taste test. Naturally, Emily would whip up a batch of her oatmeal cookies to go with it.

"It wasn't too hard considering every time Lana and I brought up something about the inn, like advertising or printed menus, you found some reason to push off the discussion." Emily turned on her griddle and buttered the bread. "It's all right, you know. Lana and I both have a lot of other commitments. And to tell you the truth, Sunni, I wasn't exactly sure how I was going to run the farm and the blog and still cook for the Cider Ridge guests."

"I know. I was asking a lot of both of you, but I just don't have the right skill set to pull off a bed and breakfast without you two. I write articles for newspapers and—" I held up the block of cheese I was holding. "I can grate cheese, too, apparently. But that's not quite enough to run an inn." It was always hard making my case (although it didn't seem that I needed to work too hard at it) without being able to mention one of the big reasons for not opening the inn. But the more I thought about it, my indecisiveness really did have more to do with me than with Edward. I was never cut out to run a bed and breakfast. There was literally nothing in my resume or my character that said cheery hostess in an apron pouring coffee and making small talk. Making beds and doing lots of laundry wasn't exactly my idea of a dream fulfilled. There were plenty of people who were born to do the job. Each of my sisters, for example. But not me.

Emily piled the cheese on the bread. The butter sizzled on the hot griddle. "First of all, you have many skills. I'm fairly certain I couldn't solve a murder, let alone even get near one, and Lana, as we both know, couldn't write her way out of a paper bag. She's far too practical for allowing thoughts and words to flow onto paper."

"I'm sure she'd have a few choice words to write to Dave if she ever decided to give him the time of day." I drifted off with a smile for a moment imagining what a salty, entertaining letter *that* would be.

Emily looked at me. "You're thinking about that letter, aren't you?"

"Yes, and I believe it would be one for the history books. Poor Lana. What a weasel."

"He sure did turn out to be just that," Emily said. She pressed her spatula down on the bread. The butter sizzled more, and the cheese began to ooze out of the sides. "But farming, Sunni? What would your raise?"

"Oh, the animals would just be for snuggling. I do like those

45

fuzzy alpacas. They look like cartoon characters. I'd keep my job. Might even start that novel I've been wanting to write since college. The farm would just be to improve my quality of life. I love what you and Nick have built here. It's a lot of work but I'm more suited to mucking out a horse stall than folding linen napkins into little swans."

"You were going to start a rustic inn, not a Michelin star restaurant, Sunni. I think swans might have been overkill."

"See, that proves my point. I don't even know how to set a proper bed and breakfast table."

Emily flipped the sandwiches. The first sides were perfectly golden. If I'd been making them they would have been charred or undercooked. "Sounds like you've made up your mind about this."

I sighed. "I think I have, Em. At least I'm ninety percent there. I just don't want to feel like a failure. After talking about little else these past few years, it sort of feels like just that."

"Nonsense," Emily said crisply. "You returned that dilapidated old manor to its former glory and that, in itself, is a big achievement."

I hugged her. "Thanks. I really needed that, Em."

CHAPTER 9

*A*dmittedly, I was somewhat relieved that Ursula and Henry had the morning off to take care of dental appointments. After Ursula's teary session at the table the morning before, I was glad to have the house to myself. I hadn't mentioned anything about not opening the inn to the Rice siblings. For some reason, I was sure they'd take it almost personally, as if they hadn't done a good enough job. Nothing could be further from the truth. The house was truly a masterpiece. As much as I would have liked to take credit for the transformation, I could only do so from a financial standpoint and from the occasional color choice. Ursula and Henry had transformed, coddled and coaxed the house back to its original beauty. That was why their connection to the Cider Ridge Inn was so profound and why the thought of no longer working within its walls so difficult to accept.

Of course, the phrase 'having the house to myself' meant something very different in my particular house.

"Wait, what's that I hear?" Edward said as he cupped his hand to his ear. "That's right. Nothing. I hear nothing, and what

47

a glorious nothing it is." He waved his arm toward the stove. His hand jumped ahead of his arm as it disappeared into vapor and then reappeared right where it should, attached to his hand. "Behold, there is no mess on the stove, no pile of egg shells in the waste basket and no odor of burning toast in the air."

I put my hands on my hips. "How do you know there's no smell of burning toast in the air?"

"Lucky guess," he said dryly.

I sat at the table with my coffee. "Did you have some favorite smells? Things you miss?"

Edward floated to the window. I'd discovered that Edward enjoyed reminiscing about his life on earth, even if not all the memories were pleasant. However, he preferred to dwell on the good ones, the ones that evoked nostalgia and comfort. I sensed he was heading to one of those memories as he stared out the window. One of his favorite memories was riding his horse across fragrant grasses and sweet clover. It wasn't just the smell of nature as his horse kicked up loamy earth, it was the feel of the wind in his face, the sense of freedom that came with riding a horse fast and hard across a field. Would having horses on the property help him relive the experience even more? Or would it sadden him to watch Jackson riding across the grass? It was hard to know if ghosts could live vicariously through someone else's experience, but it seemed we might know the answer in the near future. That thought caused a pulse of excitement to race through me. The prospect of turning this into a farm, a place with horses and possibly even cartoonish alpacas, was exciting and new, an interesting turn in my life I never would have imagined five years ago. I couldn't remember if I'd ever felt that same pulse of excitement when thinking about a future inn. That notion was always far too daunting to enjoy.

"There was a powder that Bonnie wore," Edward's deep, elegant voice lured me back from my thoughts. "It was a scent I enjoyed, a scent that reminded me of her soft touch, her warm skin. And the cook's pumpkin pudding," he paused, and I could have sworn his chest rose as if he was taking a deep breath. He was trying to revisit the aroma of pumpkin pudding. I could only help him with words.

"The sharp peppery scent of cloves and cinnamon, an aroma that hovers between spicy and sweet. One of my favorites. And the warm, earthy scent of nutmeg," I added. "Hmm, now I wish it was fall and hot cider was in this cup instead of coffee."

"Those were some of my favorites." Edward was still lost in his musings. "And the oil I used on my saddle. Most people found it pungent, but it reminded me of the hours spent in the saddle, the time spent on my horse's back, just the two of us moving across the land, searching for our next destination."

"Edward, how would it make you feel if there were horses on the property? Do you think you would enjoy it, or would it make you sad to see them knowing you couldn't ride or touch or even smell them?" Once or twice, Emily's horse, Butterscotch, had gotten loose from her pen and wandered down to the inn. I found Edward standing on the porch talking to her.

"I think just seeing them would make my heart glad. They are magnificent to watch, running in a field." His face turned my direction. "You can't possibly think you're going to make those poor animals carry around your ridiculous houseguests. Riding takes a deep understanding of the animal. I once watched a man pull so hard at his horse's mouth just to turn him down the lane that the gelding finally reared up. The rider, an absolute imbecile, slid to the ground. Then he had the nerve to get up and start beating the horse with his crop. Naturally, I stepped in to stop the man. I let him know the only beast at fault in the situation was him and that he was the one who needed the beating with a crop. I also added that I would be happy to give it to him. Needless to say, he walked off with his horse posthaste."

49

I laughed. "Sometimes, I really regret not having known you back then. I'm sure you were quite the rogue."

His face sharpened. "I was never a swindler and if anyone said as such, then they were deeply mistaken. I consider it an insult to my good name."

I lifted my hands to slow down his tirade. "Sorry, sorry, my mistake. Wrong word, I suppose. I guess I'm just used to seeing rogue being used to describe heroes in historical romances. Obviously, it doesn't translate well into nineteenth century. Just know, it was considered a compliment. However… your good name?"

He brushed off to the other side of the kitchen. His image trailed across like shooting stars crossing a night sky. "I assure you, it was in certain circles. Just not the ones my family traveled in. When would you bring horses? You have no barn or livery to house them."

"A barn could be built. It's just something I'm thinking about. Jackson loves horses, and he knows how to ride. He's quite skilled." My mind popped back to the time I was sent off in a runaway carriage by a murder suspect, and Jackson borrowed a police horse to chase after the carriage. He saved me and the carriage horses from probable death.

Edward wore a slight grin that bordered on pride. "Jackson rides? Interesting. Would not have guessed it."

"Maybe it's an inherited trait." All the talk about horses was giving me time to lead up to one major announcement. "Edward, I'm thinking I might not open the Cider Ridge Inn to guests." Granted, I took a somewhat cowardly way out with my passive phrasing, but there was still that smidgen of a possibility that I would go through with the plan. It was only that the smidgen grew smaller with each passing day.

Edward hadn't responded yet.

"Did you hear me?" I asked, not that there was any question about it.

"Yes, yes, I heard. How could that be? For the past years, all I've heard about is the Cider Ridge Inn and the guests who would be flowing through the doors to make my life miserable."

"After some long reflection and a great deal of changing my mind back and forth, I've decided innkeeper might not be the job for me."

He scoffed. "That I could have told you. The innkeepers I knew were generally squat, ruddy-faced men with little or no hair and barking voices that could be heard across the room. In my day, guests were not coddled. You were just lucky to get a room on a stormy night, and if there was still some hard tack and moldy cheese left in the kitchen you might get a meal with your cold, dusty room."

"You never ate hard tack or moldy cheese in your life," I noted.

"True, but I thought it lent a certain atmosphere to the story. It's true that in most cases the food was quite tasty, braised chicken or pork cutlets. One particular inn I stayed at often served a Yorkshire pudding that was nearly as good as the one our cook made in England. However, I stand by my physical description of the innkeeper. You do not resemble a squat, bald man by any stretch."

"Thank you and very good to know that I don't look like my Uncle Frank." We often broke into nonsense and chiding, but I needed to bring it back around to the topic. I still wasn't sure what he thought. I assumed he'd be thrilled, but as I looked at him, I realized I'd assumed wrong. "I thought you'd be pleased. All this time you've been fretting about having to stay in closets to avoid guests. You worried the two of us weren't going to be able to chat, like this, right here. Without guests—"

"But this was your dream. My existence has ruined your future," he said glumly.

"No, you haven't ruined my future. This wasn't as much a

dream as it was a business plan. For a brief moment in time, I thought I wanted out of journalism. But it's what I studied in college. It's what I love to do."

"Along with solving unseemly murders," he added.

"Yes, it's true, I wouldn't have been able to run around town chasing down murder suspects if I was here at the inn setting cookies on a tray and putting mints on pillows."

"Mints on pillows?" His dark brows scrunched together. I'd lost him again. He would spend the next few minutes trying to learn why modern folk put mints on pillows.

"It's a thing. I can't explain it or how it started, but it's often considered just a nice, homey gesture to leave a mint or chocolate on a pillow."

"Chocolate on a pillow?" he asked.

"Argh, never mind." I set my cup in the sink. "I've got to get to work. No murders this time... just flowers and parades... unfortunately."

CHAPTER 10

The door to Prudence's office was closed. I looked at Myrna for confirmation that she was inside. On the way to work, a long mental pep talk had convinced me to walk right in and ask for the lead reporter job. After all, it was mine before golden boy Dave swept in and snatched it away. If the inn was the only thing standing in the way of me getting the position, then I could tell Prudence that was no longer an impediment. I'd reached that final and definitive decision by the time I parked the jeep. It shocked me a little how easily I'd finally made the choice not to open the inn. Although, there had been a good deal of agonizing and flipping back and forth before I'd actually reached that *easy* decision.

"She's in a particularly testy mood," Myrna whispered loudly.

"We all know who we can thank for that," Parker muttered from behind his computer.

Dejectedly, I returned to my desk. My jolt of courage had all but disappeared. I needed to get Prudence in the right mood and testy didn't sound like it. Myrna was typing away on her keyboard, her long, pink nails clicking out a little beat as she filled in spreadsheets for this week's advertisements. Myrna and I had made a pact long ago that once the inn was ready to open, she could turn in her resignation from the paper and join me at the Cider Ridge Inn. Now, I'd have to let her down. I probably felt the worst about Myrna. She was looking forward to working at the inn. Not that she minded her job at the paper. Sure she complained, as most people do at one point or another about their job, but Prudence was a difficult boss. I couldn't see how the paper could possibly survive without Myrna making sure everything was running smoothly. It seemed I'd just saved Prudence a second big headache, trying to replace irreplaceable Myrna. If only I could tell Prudence that as a way to worm myself into her good graces, but there was no way I could use that as leverage. Myrna had never mentioned leaving to Prudence, and that secret was going to stay well hidden.

Somehow, my courage snapped back awake, and before I could change my mind, I hopped up and headed toward the office door. I didn't need to look at my two newsroom mates to know they were both watching with great anticipation as to whether or not the boss would invite me inside.

I knocked firmly, not too light so as to seem wimpy and not too forceful so as to seem pushy. If there was one thing Prudence didn't stand for it was pushiness.

"Come in," Prudence called from the back of the office where her finely carved mahogany desk sat in front of her velvet upholstered chair. It was a rather imperial set up, something fit for a queen or, in this case, Prudence Mortimer.

The comical thing about her royal desk setup was that the rest of the décor was whimsical with frilly polka dot arm chairs for those of us lucky enough to be invited in and her ceramic collection of frogs all lined up neatly on a bright green bookshelf.

Prudence didn't look up from her paperwork. "Please, sit, Sunni. I'll be right with you."

Normally, she would have told me she was too busy for a chat, but, at the moment, I had leverage. If I left, there would be no one to write articles for the paper. The entire paper rested solely on my keyboard, so to speak.

I sat quietly and a tad fidgety, like a kid waiting for the principal's scolding, as she finished reading whatever was in front of her.

"Now, what can I do for you?" Prudence pushed her glasses higher on her nose. "How is the Founders' Day story coming? Terrible business isn't it, Dave up and leaving so abruptly. It's lucky he'd already found a job because he certainly would not have gotten a good reference from me. Very irresponsible and after I gave him the lead reporter position." Her first question got lost in her long speech. It seemed awkward for me to get back to it without going through some of the other stuff first.

"Uh, yes, my sister was as shocked as you." Never in a million years would I have thought of bringing up Lana, but she'd thrown me off with her unexpected rant.

"That's right. The two of them were dating. Then I like him even less. I hope you're able to get what you need for the story. I realize you don't have much time."

"It shouldn't be a problem." Floats and parades just didn't take all that much time.

"I knew you could do it. I said to myself 'Prue, if anyone is up to the task it's Sunni'." She reached for a small tin of mints and offered me one.

I shook my head. "No, thanks."

She snapped the tin shut. "Well, I'm glad we had this chat. We don't get enough time to talk." She was ready to dismiss me, and the only topic that had been discussed was dreadful Dave. (I'd created the new nickname on my way to the newsroom. I was sure Lana would love it.)

"If you don't mind, Prue, I have something to ask."

She blinked at me behind her glasses. "Yes, go ahead, but make it short. I have calls to make."

I took a breath. "Yes, I'll be brief. I'd like to have the lead reporter position." There, that was brief, I thought.

"Sunni, we've talked about this before. You're going to be leaving the newspaper to run the inn. How have my niece and nephew been doing? I hope they're not driving you too crazy. Little Ursula can be such a pistol."

"They're fine and they're almost done, but here's the thing." I hadn't spoken the words out loud yet, at least not in a way that the meaning couldn't be misinterpreted. "I'm not going to open the inn to guests. It's just going to be my home. I don't want to leave my job at the paper."

She sat back with a loud puff of air. It had enough force behind it that I could smell the mint on her breath. "I'm flabbergasted, Sunni. I don't know what to say." She released one of those older society women laughs, a sound that wasn't exactly a laugh, more of a deep, mirth-filled moan. "I must say this has been a week of surprises." Her merriment gave me some hope that she was going to place me in the position without a second thought. But, as usual, I was reading the woman wrong. She sat forward and fingered the mint box, apparently considering a second one. "I've got a few out of state interviews for lead reporter lined up. But you'll be on the list for consideration."

I slumped slightly from having the wind knocked out of me. "But you know my work, Prue. You know me."

"Of course and that puts you well at the top of the list, but I'm going to need a second reporter and there are few people, locally, who have the skills or want the position. Unfortunately, most people won't relocate for a junior reporter job. They want the top post if they're going to make such a big sacrifice."

"So I can't have the position because I already live here in Firefly Junction?"

She decided against the mint and placed her hands primly on her lap. "You make my reasoning sound ridiculous." Her thin upper lip twitched. The last thing I wanted to do was anger her.

"No, I understand. You're right. I'm going to write a great article about the Founders' Day events, and you'll see that I deserve the position. Thanks for your time. I'm off to get the story. It will be filled with flowers and trumpets and all the excitement that goes along with a parade. Readers will feel as if they're sitting right there on the parade route."

The twitch disappeared, and her matronly smile returned. "That's the spirit. Remember to shut the door on your way out."

I walked out with chin up. I meant what I'd said. I would show her my worth with my words. It was hard to believe and more than a little aggravating that I once again had to prove myself, but I believed in my skills as a writer. Maybe it really was time to start that novel.

I opened the door. Myrna was busily typing away on the keyboard. I sighed. It was time to break the news about the inn to Myrna. With any luck, the conversation would go better than the one I'd just had.

CHAPTER 11

*M*yrna had taken the news as I'd expected. She put on her strongest front and told me she was happy for me and that she'd be fine, but there was a slight lip quiver that assured me she was taking it harder than she let on. Telling Myrna had been much more difficult than I thought, but she hugged me on the way out the door and told me as long as we were still working together, she was just fine. I told her I felt the same way. I only hoped that Prudence would see her way into giving me the position that I deserved.

I'd decided the best way to get the nitty-gritty details of the parade was to work right alongside the volunteers. I'd get first-hand experience of float building and hopefully learn insider details from the people who were elbow deep in rose petals.

I parked the jeep. Brandy, Sylvia's assistant, was just getting out of her small sedan. Once again, she carried a tray of coffees as she hurried into the building. There were even more cars in front of the warehouse than yesterday. The parade was tomorrow morning, so it was crunch time, like the malls on Christmas Eve.

I headed toward the building. As I crossed the vast parking

lot, I spotted Christy's assistant, Marilyn, struggling with two big boxes of donuts. I hurried across, deciding my volunteerism could start now.

"Let me help you with that."

She peered up at me over the boxes. "Oh, it's you. Sunni, right?"

"Yes, that's right." I lifted the top box off to lighten her load. It was more the unwieldiness of the boxes than the actual weight. "I was hoping I could roll up my sleeves and do a little work this morning so I could get the feel of the whole operation. Do you think they'll let me?"

"Uh, sure, you'll have to sign a waiver, of course. Sylvia is a real stickler for legal forms and what not."

"Understandable. I noticed some of the volunteers standing up on high ladders to get to the tops of the floats. If needed, I can climb a ladder or two. I'm a pretty good tree climber by nature."

Marilyn chuckled. "Then I'm going to insist you work with us on the pony. We're all afraid of heights. We've been pulling straws to see who gets to make the climb. Although, we've been using coffee stirrers instead of straws. I pulled the short stirrer this morning, which is why I had to make a donut run."

We stepped onto the concrete pathway that led to the door. Just a few feet before we reached the building, the door burst open and a man stomped out. He was tall, over six feet, with thick, dark hair and a small paunch. He looked slightly familiar, but I couldn't remember where I'd seen him. He was one of those men some women would find attractive, but I thought he just looked mean. And angry. He was grumbling to himself as he stormed past, not even acknowledging the fact that if we'd taken a few quicker steps, the door would have smacked both of us right in the *donuts.*

Marilyn and I were rather stunned by the near miss. We

watched as he marched with heavy feet across the asphalt parking lot and climbed into a gray sedan.

"That sure was rude," I said.

"That's Arthur Andrews. He's always a grumpy sort. Especially since Sylvia kicked him off the Founders' Day Committee."

There it was again, my chance to get some dirty laundry on Founders' Day, and there I was again, unable to use it due to Prudence's silly notion of what people liked to read.

"Why was he kicked off?" I asked casually, as a friend and not a reporter. At least that was the effect I was going for.

"Who knows? Sylvia is always finding fault with everyone."

My posture deflated. It seemed I wasn't going to get a juicy nugget, even with my good deed of donut carrying.

We continued toward the door, both of us pausing out of caution before I reached for the handle.

"Why was he here?" I asked, not ready to surrender yet. "If he's no longer on the committee."

"Most likely to see Christy. They're dating. That's probably why Sylvia fired him. The whole rivalry thing." Much better answer than the first one. Seemed there was quite a bit of drama going on behind the scenes at float production.

CHAPTER 12

The mouthwatering aroma of donuts circled my head as Marilyn and I negotiated our way through the flurry of activity. The air was thick with flowery fragrance and heated tension. People were rushing around, petals were flying and glue guns were being wielded like we'd just been dropped into the Wild West. To my untrained eye, the floats looked a little more wilted than the day before. I could only imagine how hard it was to create something so detailed and complex in a time crunch and, at the same time, frantically, keep it from withering away to dust.

"These people are not messing around," I said.

"You noticed?" Marilyn took a quick turn, donuts and all, to avoid Benny wheeling a trash can dolly through the maze. "Everyone wants to win first prize. It helps get you on the volunteer list next year if you worked on the award winning float. The city council members will be judging the floats on originality, color and workmanship."

I snapped my face her direction, the first time I'd pulled my laser vision from the pandemonium in front of me. "That's where

I've seen Arthur Andrews, the rude man who nearly ran us over. He was on the city council."

"That's right. He was treasurer. But not anymore. He got voted out."

"I think I remember there was an active push to remove him, even before his term was up. If today's encounter is any indication of his personality, I can see why there was such a concerted effort."

"He's not always that angry. I can only assume he ran into Sylvia on his way out of the warehouse." We had nearly reached the gigantic pink and yellow pony when someone started yelling. It was a much more alarmed tone than the normal shouting in the building.

"We've been sabotaged!" someone yelled.

Marilyn nearly dropped her donuts. "That's Christy. Something's happened." She took off. I followed closely at her heels. We placed the donut boxes on a work table and circled around the float to the hind quarters of the pony where all the excitement seemed to be.

Christy's face was red with rage. The pony volunteers, clad in their cute matching aprons, all gathered around her. The focus of their attention was the tail of the pony. It had been draped in yellow rose petals and feathery green ferns were pleated in between the rows of petals. As we drew closer, the sabotage came into view. A large swath of the tail had been smashed in. The chicken wire frame for the tail was caved in, and all the petals had been torn off.

The group of volunteers muttered amongst themselves. The name *Sylvia* came up more than once. And then, as if she'd heard her name from all the way across the room, the project manager arrived with her own personal entourage, including Brandy, as if she was a member of royalty. The imperious expression she wore above the high collar of her tight knit blouse and diamond neck-lace only added to the look.

"What's going on here?" she asked. "What's happened?"

Christy emerged from the stunned, distraught group with a scowl that was sharp enough to carve a pumpkin. She didn't let the old rule of etiquette about pointing stop her from shoving her finger right in Sylvia's face. The way Sylvia stared down at the finger, I half expected her to bite it off. Instead, she pushed Christy's hand out of the way.

"I see your manners are as crude as ever, Christy," Sylvia sneered. "What has everyone here in such a lather? Or did you all just realize how ridiculous this pony float was?" For someone who was in charge of the entire event, she sure didn't believe in being a team player.

"You sabotaged this float. We've been working on the mane all morning and hadn't been paying attention to the rear of the float." Christy's face grew dark pink as she spoke, and a bit of spittle sprayed from her mouth. "Someone bashed in our tail. I know it was you."

"You can't just accuse her," Brandy spoke up sternly though her body language showed she was nervous about sticking her neck out. "Besides, she's been with me this last hour."

That struck me as a lie since I saw Brandy returning with coffee as I pulled into the parking lot. It seemed she was willing to step out on a limb for her boss. I just couldn't understand why.

Sylvia crossed her arms and lifted her chin even higher. Soon she'd be staring straight up at the ceiling. "How dare you accuse me? I'm sure it was just one of your clumsy assistants." That comment rightfully earned some scowls and defensive words from the pony volunteers. Did Sylvia walk over with her support team because she knew exactly what she'd be facing down when she reached the pony? She marched over pretending to find out what was going on, something you could expect from the person running the whole event, but why bring along the troops?

Christy crossed her arms too, only tighter and more angrily than Sylvia. "No one on my team did this. We were all working up at the front. It was you or one of your volunteers, and there's nothing you can say—" Christy looked harshly at Brandy. "And there's nothing your little scared sheep can say that will change my mind. You know we're going to win, so you decided to resort to drastic measures."

Sylvia's harsh laugh shot out like shards of glass. "I'm sorry but this silly pony has no chance of winning."

Brandy had stuck her neck out, but Sylvia couldn't even be bothered to stand up for her. I glanced back to see how she was taking this whole argument after standing up for Sylvia and even going so far as to make up a fake alibi. She was still standing firm, brows furrowed and round little fists clenched as if she was ready to go to battle for Sylvia.

"Well, looks like you and your team have work to do, so we'll leave you to it." Sylvia turned and her team turned with her in near perfect unison. She had the royalty thing down pat.

Christy didn't look too receptive to some outsider, especially a journalist, at the moment, so I decided to tag, inconspicuously as possible, along with Sylvia's group. I was curious to know what they'd be talking about once they got back to their side of the warehouse. I heard several volunteers muttering about whether or not Sylvia actually did sabotage the float. It seemed they knew her well enough to consider it. I certainly did, and I'd only met her briefly.

Brandy was doing her usual lady-in-waiting routine as she stuck close by her queen's side. Sylvia was working her hardest to not look distraught about being accused in front of the whole team, but her hard veneer had cracked. She looked less confident than usual. That didn't stop her from clapping loudly and lecturing her team for dawdling.

"Team Dragon, we have less than twenty-four hours. We can't let anything distract us from the task at hand. Let's get back to work."

Brandy had answered a phone call. She finished as Sylvia completed her little team spirit talk. "Sylvia, that was Beatrice Georgio, the artist who designed the dragon. She has a terrible cold and will not be able to ride along on the float."

Sylvia released a sigh that could be heard through the clamor in the building. "Who will we get at such short notice? Every float has to have four riders." Some of the volunteers began talking amongst themselves as if trying to decide who would get the honor. It seemed fitting that if the artist couldn't make it, someone who at least had a hand in decorating it should ride along.

Brandy raised her hand hesitantly. "Sylvia, it's always been a dream of mine to ride on a parade float." Her hopeful smile at the end of her little speech was so cute only a cold-hearted person could say no. Sylvia was about as ice queen as they got, but, even I, didn't anticipate her response.

First, there was the signature cackle, then she placed a hand on Brandy's shoulder. But it wasn't a kind touch. It was a 'you're so pathetic' one. "I'm sorry but there's a weight limit on the float." Brandy looked as if someone had literally swept her legs out from under her. A few volunteers hid amused smiles, but most of them looked truly aghast. As I was. I decided right then that I no longer wanted anything to do with Sylvia Franco, and if she thought she was going to be praised or quoted in my story, she was sorely mistaken.

I'd come to volunteer, and there was at least one team that was now behind and might need an extra hand. I headed over to the giant pink and yellow pony.

CHAPTER 13

*C*hristy's attitude was much more generous towards me
when I volunteered to help. She even handed me one of
her customized aprons. Not that I was allowed to actually apply
petals, leaves or seeds. Those tasks were left to the more seasoned
veterans. But I made myself useful by fetching supplies, sorting
seeds and trimming off the nice looking leaves from stems.

Most of the small talk was about where to place petals and
other frilly things that belonged on the pony, but the occasional
complaint about Sylvia Franco crept into the conversation. It
seemed that most everyone was convinced that Sylvia had sabotaged their float. Several of the more skilled volunteers, along
with Christy, had set right to work repairing the damage. Pliers,
pruning shears and floral wire were used to restore the tail to its
former shape and size. The floral additions would cover any
flaws. They had to work fast to get the whole lush tail back in
shape. They were more determined than ever to present the best
float and win that coveted award. The phrases 'Sylvia will have a
stroke' and 'Sylvia will drop dead with jealousy' were being

bandied about. After seeing Sylvia in her true form, I was rooting for the pony to take the trophy.

Marilyn had finished some detailing on the shiny hooves, and she came over to see how I was getting along. "We sure were lucky to get your help today."

"I was glad to do it. It's given me a lot of journalistic insight into just how much work goes into one of these floats. As a parade watcher, you *ooh* and *aww* and marvel at how pretty they are, but it's easy to forget that dozens of people spent days to create each masterpiece."

"Those of us who work on these floats are always very proud to see our creations and hard work drift down the street earning applause and cheers from the spectators. Would you like to see the inside of the float? You can stand under the base where the car will be located. I can show you how it all works."

"Sure. That would be great." I was surprised how interesting I was finding the whole thing. Maybe it wouldn't be such a dull article after all. I planned to focus on the volunteer aspect and how seriously they took their jobs and how labor intensive the whole thing was. They were the true heroes in this. The woman in charge of the whole event wouldn't even get a mention if I had my way.

Marilyn walked me around to the side of the float. The sixteen foot tall pony was standing on a flat rectangular base that was covered with orange rose petals and brown bark. Several chairs for the float riders had been set up at the base of his front hooves. Christy, the pony artist and two of the volunteers would be riding along with the pony, waving to the crowd as it *pranced* proudly past.

Marilyn looked at me. "You're tall. You'll definitely have to duck down to get inside." As she said it, a secret door peeled away from the base and the empty inside of the float was revealed. I leaned over but kept my head up to take a look around. I noticed only a few threads of light as I surveyed the empty cavity. "As you can see, it's big enough for a mid-sized car. Ralph Barrett, the local mechanic, will be driving the float down the parade route."

We moved awkwardly across to what my sense of direction told me was the front of the horse. It was pretty hard to tell for certain once we were inside and the door was mostly shut. My neck and back were beginning to tighten from the hunched over, neck craning position.

"It must be terribly dark in here when that door is completely shut," I said.

Right then, a sharp beam of light shot through a flap that Marilyn popped open. "This is what we call the peephole. It allows the driver to see out to the white line that's been drawn along the parade route. As long as they stay square over the middle of that line, they won't hit anything."

I peered through the slot. It didn't allow for any of the peripheral vision one used when driving a car. "Guess it takes nerves of steel to drive with a massive pony and people counting on you to get them safely to the finish line."

Marilyn laughed. "They're only going three miles per hour, so it's not too stressful. Of course, there have been mishaps with the occasional spectator walking out to get a closer picture and stepping into the space needed for clearance. I wasn't around but I did hear that about ten years ago a float came to an abrupt stop when the driver got drowsy and accidentally stepped on the brake. A woman was tossed off, but she managed to land mostly on her feet." I took a moment in the dark box to visualize Sylvia getting bounced off her float. I kept the smile to myself and continued my tour, short and awkward and uncomfortable as it was.

"Follow me to this side." Marilyn, who was a good five inches shorter, was having a much easier time moving about. Twice, I grazed my head on the wooden frame above me. I had to bend my knees to avoid bumping it altogether.

Myrna pushed her hand through a hole at the rear. A two by two flap opened up. It was much larger and reminded me a bit of the rear flap on a pair of long johns. "This is where the exhaust goes out and the fresh air comes in. These are pretty air tight otherwise. As you might have noticed"—She smiled—"I noticed you rubbing your head a few times. This base is constructed out of wood, two by fours and plywood. The pony above us is made mostly of air but when you add the organic materials and glue it starts to get heavy. The base needs to be strong enough to support the float and the people riding on it."

"I'm no engineer but that makes sense. It is massive." I was relieved to be leaving the cramped box. My legs wobbled a little as I stooped down lower to get out through the short door. "Has Christy calmed down about the tail incident?" I asked.

Marilyn did a quick glance around to make sure Christy wasn't in hearing distance. "She's still stewing about it. She's asked several volunteers to stay the night to make sure no one messes with it again. It has to be ready in the morning or else we'll be disqualified."

"It's too bad someone has to stay here, but I don't blame her. Like you said, it has to be ready in the morning."

"George and Carl, the two college boys, they're going to bring their sleeping bags and snacks. I think they're looking kind of forward to it. There's only one thing in the way."

I nodded. "Let me guess. Sylvia?"

"Yes. She would never allow it. You saw the waiver you had to sign. She's very big on following protocols." Marilyn moved closer to lower her voice. "They're going to hide in the men's restroom until she locks up. Now, if you don't mind walking with me to the supply closet, I need to get some more floral wire. Christy wants to add a few details to the base of the float."

"My pleasure. Thank you for the tour. Now, when I'm watching the parade, I'll know exactly what's going on under the pony."

CHAPTER 14

*A*fter a long morning of sorting seeds and holding leaves, I headed to Lana's with a box of her favorite bakery brownies. She was outside watering the hydrangea bushes that bordered the front of the house.

She still looked rather disheveled with her hair pushed under a red bandana scarf and no makeup, but she smiled when she saw me climb out of the jeep. (It might have been the bakery box, but I was going to let myself believe it was me.)

"Look at you all hip and rugged and watering flowers." I lifted up the box. "Your favorite German chocolate brownies."

Her lip turned up at the edge.

I lowered the box. "Not exactly the response I was expecting. Too soon after the cookie debacle?"

Lana shut off the hose. "I think I'm off anything sweet or chocolatey for at least a month."

"Chocolate lightweight. I could have downed that package—possibly not without the milk but I digress—and woken the next morning craving a chocolate croissant."

Lana looked over at me as we climbed her front steps. "You say that with such pride."

"Yep. So... I've made my decision." I said it as the screen door snapped shut behind us.

Lana stopped and turned. "You mean the inn?"

"Yes. It came to me on the way to work and that led to a whole domino of events, including me asking for my lead reporter job back."

"So, you've decided not to open it." Lana was wearing the same let down expression Myrna had worn when I first told her.

"Yes, I'm sorry. I thought that was a given when I said I'd made a decision."

"Not a given. I guess I still held out a little hope that you were going to go for it." Lana continued on to the kitchen. I walked dejectedly behind her, suddenly the little sister again, the one who decided not to be in the school play that Lana and her friends were producing. I'd let her down.

"I thought you were willing to support me no matter what I decided."

We stepped into her kitchen. There was a pile of flyers on the table.

"If you've got a little time, I need help folding these flyers. I'm handing them out at the Founders' Day event. All the businesses do it. It's a cheap form of advertising."

I sat down hard, still feeling the sting of her obvious disappointment. Growing up it had always been far worse to disappoint Lana than our parents. Mostly because Mom and Dad were too busy to worry about the little things going on in my life. But Lana always kept track and she always let me know, with no uncertainty, when I was making a bad decision. Sometimes I took her advice and sometimes I ignored her and asserted my little sister independence. Usually, and annoyingly, it turned out she was right in the end. But not this time. I could feel my decision in my bones. I knew I'd made the right one.

"I thought you would be behind me on this," I said, ignoring her little speech about the flyers.

Lana divided the stack in half and pushed one pile toward me. "Just fold them in thirds. I'm going to add a cute paperclip afterward."

"See and that is why I'm not cut out for running the inn. Not only would I just hand these out as is, if I'd even decided to make a flyer, I would never think of adding a cute paperclip. No one's going to toss a flyer that has a cute paperclip attached."

"You act as if Emi and I were going to throw you into this alone. We would have been with you every step of the way."

I absently folded the paper into thirds. It was always a rather subjective paper fold because you had to start by guessing where the first third was then hope the other side matched up. My first attempt was less than precise.

"Do you need me to make you one first, so you can use it as a guide?" Lana started folding one. Of course, it was perfect. Again, I pictured myself trying to fold linen napkins for a guest table. It didn't go well.

I pushed the pile of flyers away. "When we spoke about this yesterday, you mentioned some relief at the notion of me not opening the inn. You and Emily are both so busy with your own jobs, how could you possibly have time to help? Besides, I spoke to Emily and she was just as glad not to have to cook at the inn. Her life is full enough. This whole thing was your idea." Yes, I was going that route, but she sort of deserved it and it was more than partially true.

"My idea?" Lana looked up but didn't miss a beat on the paper folding. She kept folding perfect thirds without even looking at the flyers.

"You put the idea into my head. 'Oh, Sunni, you could make

the house fabulous and guests would be lining up to stay at the Cider Ridge Inn.'" I used my Lana impression, but she was not *impressed*.

She put on her big sister condescending smile. "Just make sure you're making the right decision. You've always been impulsive."

I blinked at her over the stack of flyers. "There's nothing wrong with being impulsive. Just because you plan out every minute of your day. Then you wonder why you can't keep a guy. They all like a little impulsiveness, you know?" By the time I'd finished, I was in full regret mode, especially given the hurt expression staring back at me. "I'm sorry, Lana. I didn't mean that. Dave was a jerk."

"No, no you're right, little sister." She always used the phrase little sister in a moment of tension just to remind me who'd been on Earth longer and how that automatically transferred to her being wiser in all life matters. "I can't keep a man, and maybe that's for the best. And if you don't see yourself running an inn, then it's good you made the decision now before the plan got too far."

"The entire remodel happened already." I wasn't helping my own case, but it seemed I was finally talking about this out loud, with my sister as a sounding board. Although, she was more of a talking board, but it was a good thing. I'd made this large decision mostly in my own mind. There had definitely been some lively debates between the skeptical Sunni and the 'you can do this, girl' Sunni, but in the end, I was only talking to myself. If there was anyone who could force me to really look at my decision, it was Lana. I was now blaming our first conversation, where she seemed far more supportive and less a big sister, on the fact that she'd just been dumped and had consumed an inordinate amount of cookies.

Lana shrugged. "So now you just have a really nice, really big house." She tapped her pile of flyers to remind me to get back to work. Reluctantly, I picked up a flyer. I'd planned to just stop by with some brownies, check on my sister (clearly, she was her old self again) and then get back to work. Now, I was in new turmoil about a decision I was very certain about just a few hours earlier.

I sat back with a slump. "My gosh, it's the whole travel team or school team dilemma all over again."

A smile tilted her mouth. "I forgot about that big controversy."

I sat forward again and hastily folded a flyer. "It wasn't a controversy until you stepped in. I'd made my mind up to play for the travel softball team instead of the school team. They were going to go out of state and do all kinds of cool trips, then you put the little bug in my ear that I was letting my whole school down and that people wouldn't like me anymore."

She lifted a neatly folded flyer. "Like this." She pointed to the one I'd just finished. "Not like that. I was right about that and you know it."

"I don't know because I ended up playing for the school, thus missing out on some cool traveling not to mention being able to play with different teammates from around the county."

"I was right though."

I grunted. "Boy, oh boy, heartbreak doesn't last long in that steel-cased heart of yours. Lana, I want to be a journalist. I want to write that novel that's been floating in my head all these years. I don't want to cater to a bunch of strangers. Besides, having guests at the inn will disrupt—" I sucked in a breath and glued my lips shut.

The sudden stop in conversation was actually profound enough that Lana stopped folding. She looked up at me. "Disrupt what?"

"Huh?" Playing dumb was the only thing that came to mind after the stressful conversation.

"You said 'besides, having guests at the inn will disrupt'. Then you stopped and you did that funny thing with your lips you do when you worry you've said too much or the wrong thing."

"Oh that. I just meant it will disrupt my life to have guests staying at the inn."

Lana laughed. "Yes, I'd say it might be a bit of a disruption. All right, I've thrown you for a big loop today. Just make the decision that's right for you. How is the Founders' Day story going?"

I was just as glad to switch topics. "It's not without turmoil. Today, I helped a woman named Christy Jacobs and her team of volunteers finish decorating a sixteen foot tall pony. Sylvia Franco, the project manager, had apparently sabotaged Christy's float because it's some big competition."

Lana nodded. "Ah yes, the Franco, Jacobs feud."

I sat up straighter. "Wait, do you know them?"

"Not closely but I put on a wedding reception for Christy's older daughter. At the time, there was some big scandal happening at the school. Christy's high school aged daughter was in competition with Sylvia's daughter for head cheerleader. I don't know the details, but I think it got pretty ugly."

"That doesn't surprise me after watching the two women in action. It's obvious they hate each other."

"Are you going to write about the rivalry in the paper?" she asked. "Seems like great reading to me."

"Most readers would think the same, but Prudence doesn't like controversy. She wants pretty girls in dresses, luncheons with small tea sandwiches and everyone always walking around with stars in their eyes."

"Since none of that sounds like you, why don't you write the piece the way you want?"

"I'm considering it but since I'm trying to wiggle my way to the lead reporter position, I thought the less rebellious plan might work better. Prue is set in her ways. She likes what she likes, no matter how much it sells papers. I did get nice heartfelt stories from some of the volunteers I worked with. I might stick with those. Unless something more noteworthy than a head cheerleader rivalry comes up. And with that, I think I'll head home to start on some of those heartfelt stories." I pushed the pile of flyers back toward her. "Sorry I wasn't much help with this."

"It's all right. I didn't expect much."

I laughed dryly. "Yep, big sister is back. That didn't take long at all."

CHAPTER 15

J was glad to come home to a quiet house. Now that they were reaching the end of the remodel, Ursula and Henry were spending more time at other jobs. On my way back from Lana's, I once again solidified my decision not to open the inn, even though my sister had tossed a few seeds of doubt my way. I was sure the second my big house came into view. It was still surrounded by a great deal of untamed property. Rather than the neatly trimmed boxwoods, walking paths and rose gardens I'd planned, I was envisioning a charming red barn, a few animal pens and a big vegetable garden. It was such an entirely different landscape than the one I'd been considering for the inn, it gave me a thrill. There were so many possibilities. It felt as if I was starting all over. And the vision of Jackson sitting tall on a black horse with a cowboy hat pulled low over his eyes made the whole thing that much more exciting.

Edward was out on the porch throwing the ball for Newman. Redford trotted down from the porch to greet me, but Newman was far too involved with his game. A game of fetch from the porch was another activity that would have been cancelled with guests in the house. A dog catching a ball was nothing out of the ordinary, but having the ball shoot out from no apparent source was another thing altogether.

Newman reached the front stoop the same time as me. He was breathing so hard, he could barely hold on to the ball wedged between his teeth. "I think he's had enough. Ursula texted that they were stopping work early."

"It's been a pleasurable afternoon," Edward said in a rare positive moment. "You're certain?"

"Yes, they said they were finished and had to wait for some molding to come in at the hardware store."

Edward whisked across the stoop and disappeared through the front wall. Newman and I walked inside to find him hanging around the entryway. "Not about the hammer-wielding banshee. Are you certain about the inn? Or have you changed your mind?" There was just enough angst in his tone to assure me at least one person was entirely on board with my decision. When I first broke the news he was worried that he had been the cause of me shredding my future dreams. While he'd had some part in it, he wasn't the sole reason. And the more I reflected on it, they weren't really dreams at all.

"I have to say, my sister Lana had me on the fence again, but only for a second."

"Ah yes, the high-handed business woman. That makes sense."

"Lana isn't high-handed. She's just extremely confident and set in her ways. All right, she's a little high-handed. That's only because she is the big sister, and she still hasn't shaken that whole I'm older than you so I get to boss you around privilege that comes with being born first. After sitting with her and enduring her guilt trip, I wavered and thought maybe I was making the wrong choice. Lana can be very convincing. I even went back and forth on my drive home. Was I going to regret this? Should I

79

at least give it a try? What if it turned out I was pretty good at being a hostess? Then I had a good laugh because I'm not a hostess. Sure, I can serve up a dinner to guests—"

"Good lord, woman, are you opening the inn or not!" His voice boomed through the house.

I stared at him as he fidgeted first with his waistcoat, then with the ribbon at the back of his neck. There was nothing more adorable than an embarrassed ghost. "I apologize. I make it a point to never raise my voice in front of a lady."

"Nice to be called a lady. And just to clear the air—I am not going to open the inn. At least not any time in the near future. I figure the house is here if I decide to go forward with it, but my head and heart are not in the right place for it now."

I went into the kitchen for a snack and to do a little research. After the unfriendly brush with Arthur Andrews this morning, I was curious to find out why he left the city council. Since he seemed to be in some way or another connected to both Sylvia and Christy, I thought a little research could shine some light on the whole trio. Did Sylvia kick him off of the Founders' Day Committee because she was jealous of his relationship with Christy? It seemed a terribly petty way to run a committee but then I had witnessed Sylvia in some extremely petty moments. She was treating the float contest as if it was the World Series or Super Bowl of parades. And Lana learned of the rivalry between the two women just by being the party planner for Christy's daughter's wedding. It must run long and deep. So much so that it seemed this morning's incident was not going to be the end of the shenanigans. What if Christy was leaving the two volunteers behind so they could do damage to the dragon? Would Christy stoop so low?

A slice of toast with peanut butter was the perfect late afternoon snack to go with my research. Edward was floating around the room as if he was even less affected by gravity than usual, which was saying something. He hummed a little too. It seemed I'd made him very happy.

When someone had a seat on city council, it was fairly easy to find out information. Only none of it was terrible interesting. Arthur Andrews had sat on the Firefly Junction City Council as treasurer for eight years. Last year, he was trounced in the local election (my phrase, the article in the local paper was a little gentler calling it a significant loss). There was no mention of scandal, only that there was a grassroots effort to unseat him. I clicked through some pages and had to back up when I skipped over something that caught my eye on its way out. It was a photo of Arthur Andrews at a town meeting. Sitting against the back wall, behind the seated council was none other than Sylvia Franco. She had a desk with stacks of papers and folders in front of her.

It seemed it was time to do a little research on the very disagreeable project manager. I typed in the name Sylvia Franco. After a few entries about other Sylvia Francos, I found an article about *the* Sylvia Franco. I smiled to myself thinking how much the woman would love to be called *the* Sylvia Franco. I'd only recently met and had a few interactions with her, but I already knew her top to bottom, inside out. She'd received high praise from the mayor and city council for her work at city hall. She was leaving her position as council assistant to work with the city planner. The article was several years old. A few entries later, an article praised her work with the city planner. It seemed when she was at work she was all business, and the real Sylvia stayed zipped up in the professional Sylvia. Either that or she had a lot of people snowed because her work on the Founders' Day parade was anything but praiseworthy. However, I was being hasty in my judgment. I supposed tomorrow's parade would show just how well she pulled it all together, despite being verbally abusive to her assistant and sabotaging a competitor's float.

"Horses would be nice," Edward said from somewhere in the room. I looked around and found him standing at the back door. He spun back to me. "But they must be quality steeds. None of those rundown farm mares like your sister's horse."

I sat up straight. "Excuse me but Butterscotch is one of the most magnificent horses ever to prance across a field."

"You, my dear, are no judge of horseflesh."

"Maybe not but I know what I like and I like Butterscotch."

He swept closer. "It is true that she has a gentle disposition and good nature about her, but she's hardly a horse one can gallop across a field or jump over a fence." It seemed that Edward had been dreaming about horses and riding again. Would having horses in the yard be too hard on him? It would be like a kid in a candy store who was told by his mother he couldn't actually have any of the candy.

I closed the computer and looked up at him. "Edward, I'm glad this decision is going to work out better for you."

"I am as well."

CHAPTER 16

I expected a lot of chaos when I arrived at the warehouse, but I never expected complete pandemonium. At least, that was what it looked like to my untrained eye. Apparently, it was exactly what the parade veterans had anticipated. Floats had been placed on flat dollies. Each one was slowly pulled out of the warehouse by the teams. From there, rear ends were lifted and cars were driven carefully into position. The float was then strapped onto the vehicle. The starting line for the entire parade was conveniently located about a hundred yards from the warehouse exit.

High school bands were streaming out of buses in their school colors and uniforms. The occasional honk of a trumpet or boom of a drum added to the discord. Two trailers of beautiful horses, one pair black as night and the other pair buttery gold Palominos, had pulled into the far end of the parking lot to get their horses ready for the parade. Four sets of bleachers had been set up along the parade route. Spectators were lining up on the sidewalks, anxious for the festivities to begin. A special grand-stand with colorful streamers and banners had been set up for the judges, the city council members. People dressed like fireflies, with light up gold wings, were wheeling cookie and coffee carts along the street. If Sylvia had been in charge of all this, then I had to give her credit (as much as I hated to) for a job well done. It seemed the parade was going to go off without a hitch.

Benny, the all around handyman, pulled into the parking lot in an old Chevy Impala. It was cherry red with shiny rims. I headed over to ask him about the car and how he was feeling since he would be driving the dragon through the parade.

He was wearing a shirt that had a photo of the red Impala.

"Is this yours?" I asked. "She's beautiful."

Benny's shiny silver front tooth glinted in the morning sun. In addition to everything seemingly running smoothly, we were going to have great weather. "I found her sitting in a field when I was driving through Mississippi. Offered the guy what I had in my pocket and he accepted." He patted the top of the car like I might pat one of the dogs. This car was his best friend. "It's taken a few years to get her in tip top shape, but she was worth the time and money."

It was exactly how I felt about the Cider Ridge Inn. I'd spent a lot of money to get it ready for guests, but I was just as proud to have saved it from ruin.

"How are you feeling about driving the lead float?" I asked.

"It's fine. Not my first time but each time is fun. I wouldn't miss it for the world."

"Brandy!" I recognized Sylvia's screech without even looking her way. "Has anyone seen Brandy?" she yelled but everyone was far too engaged in their own pre-parade excitement to pay attention.

Benny shook his head. "I better get in there. She looks as if she's about to chop off some heads."

I followed behind and navigated my way through the rush of people dashing in and out of the building. In the distance, the clamor of excited voices and the occasional discordant toot on a trumpet or bugle added to the general state of confusion.

Sylvia had found Brandy, unfortunately. In true form, Sylvia was berating her for something. Brandy stood steadfastly by shaking her head and, at the same time, blinking her eyes as if she might cry at any moment. Sylvia dismissed her with a rude wave of her hand and then busily texted someone. Her fingers flew over the screen at a speed that I'd only ever seen teenagers manage. Even though she was harried and tense, presumably anyone would be at a time like this, Sylvia managed to look sleek and stylish in a pink pantsuit and pearl earrings.

I was standing in the midst of the chaos, basically invisible as everyone rushed around me. I wasn't entirely sure why I'd decided to show up except that I wanted a last minute behind-the-scenes look at the whole event. I was determined to hand in a well-researched story so that Prudence could see that I was serious about taking over as lead reporter. I took a step to the side to avoid Benny moving a dolly stacked with water bottles through the room. He gave me a cursory nod. We'd bonded a moment over the Impala. I was planning to mention both Benny and his prized car in the article.

I stepped aside again for several people rushing through the building with a bag of seeds and a glue gun, an emergency patch job, apparently. As I moved out of their way, I stepped right into someone's path. "Oh, I'm so sorry." It was Brandy.

She no longer looked on the verge of tears and was back to smiling. She was amazingly resilient. "No problem. Are you still getting story details? I'm afraid this is sort of a busy time. You probably won't be able to get much interview time this morning."

I glanced across to where Sylvia had just finished a phone call. She tried to slip her phone into her pocket but seemed to realize, with a great deal of consternation, that the pockets on the slim fitting coat were just for show. She practically smacked her phone down on the work table before hurrying off in the crowd.

"Your boss looks a little stressed," I noted.

Brandy laughed dryly. "Who wouldn't be? If this whole thing goes off smoothly, she'll be promoted to assistant city planner. It's a big deal and something she's been wanting for a long time. I apologize but I really must go. I need to let the horse riders know that Sylvia wants someone picking up after the horses. Otherwise, the band members march through it and it's a whole mess."

I nodded. "Yes, I can see where that would be a problem. I'll let you go. And good luck."

I was just in the way inside the busy building, so I decided to go back outside and watch how the whole thing came together. It seemed we were going to have a wonderful parade.

CHAPTER 17

*C*ars had been driven into their 'float boxes'. I'd termed the phrase myself because no one else had a good word for it. Benny had driven his Impala underneath the dragon and strapped the back flap shut so that it didn't bounce up and down during the parade. He was just as quickly called away again.

I hung out for an hour, watching as all the band uniforms and instruments were checked. The kids had been asked to line up far ahead of the start. They'd stood in perfect array, with trumpets and drums at the ready for the first half hour, but they were starting to get antsy. The band leader was shouting at his group not to break ranks. But they were too excited and, at the same time, too bored from waiting to pay much attention.

A whistle blew. It was Brandy. Her cheeks rounded as she blew once more. Sylvia stepped forward with a megaphone. "I need all float drivers in their cars. We're going to head over to the start and get lined up. Benny," she called extra loud. "The dragon is first, right after the mayor's car." There was a pause and everyone glanced around for Benny. "Benny!" Sylvia shouted into the megaphone. Everyone flinched at the harsh noise that came out. "Has anyone seen Benny?" she called again.

Brandy said something to her and scurried into the warehouse, presumably to find Benny. Sylvia was one of those people who really thrived on having a megaphone in her hand. She went on to boss everyone around for a good ten minutes until Brandy emerged from the warehouse without Benny.

Sylvia lowered the megaphone, but it was still easy to hear her, especially since she was sort of shrieking. It seemed she'd hit her first real snafu of the morning. "Then I'll have to drive the car over to the start. We can't wait any longer. Send Benny over once you find him. He's going to get an earful from me."

The other drivers were in their cars. Each float had two team members waiting outside the float in view of the peephole to lead the float around to the staging area where they would wait until it was their turn to join the parade. The dragon, complete with red and orange rose petal flames shooting from its nostrils, spun around sharply. Sylvia was not happy, and she was driving the massive and somewhat delicate float as if someone had just cut her off and she was planning to teach them a lesson. The two team members leading her around seemed a little scared about having an angry Sylvia behind the wheel. They were staying well clear of the dragon. A few petals floated off the top of the dragon's head as Sylvia hit a pothole in the parking lot. After some maneuvering, she managed to get the unwieldy float to the starting line right behind the convertible vintage Cadillac that would be carrying the mayor and his wife.

I decided to head off and buy a hot churro. I hadn't eaten one of the greasy, doughy sticks in years, and the smell of cinnamon was luring me in. I was just enjoying the first bites when Jackson texted.

"How is the parade?" he asked.

I finished my long, sugary snack before texting back. "It

hasn't started yet, but the parade route is filled with people and the VIPs are sitting in the grandstand."

"I'd rather be there than sitting in my office finishing a report. Lunch maybe?"

"Sounds good." I texted back.

The churro was sitting like a lump of greasy dough in my stomach. I decided to take a stroll to help dissolve it. I quickly discovered the sidewalks were far too crowded for a stroll, and the parade helpers were no longer allowing anyone on the street. Since just moments before people had still been crossing back and forth, chatting with neighbors and flagging down the goodie carts, I could only assume the new sweep to clear the road meant the parade was actually going to start.

I headed back toward the center of activity, the warehouse parking lot. There was no sign of Sylvia, but I spotted Brandy talking to a few of the other volunteers. Their conversation ended just as I reached them.

"I guess it's almost show time," I said cheerily.

Brandy glanced at her watch. "Yes, there's been a few delays, but the floats are ready and the bands are getting so antsy they're about to start dancing. This happens every year. I'm sure Sylvia doesn't mind driving the float. It gives her a great perspective of the whole parade. She can see all the smiling faces as she drives past."

"Wait. You never found Benny?"

Brandy shook her head. "Can't find him anywhere, and he's not answering his phone but then that's not too odd because he hates to carry his phone. It's always sitting on his cart."

How could they possibly have lost Benny? "Did you find his cart? He should be easy to find now that things are calming down." I seemed to be far more worried than Brandy about Benny's disappearance.

"His cart is inside the building, but there's no sign of Benny."

She laughed. "He probably just found some of his car friends standing in the crowd, went off to talk to them and forgot all about the time."

The whole explanation would have sounded plausible if not for the fact that Benny was expected to drive the dragon through the parade. Surely, if the parade was about to start and the dragon was the first float, it would have occurred to Benny that it was time for him to be inside and behind the wheel. But since I didn't know Benny as well as Brandy and she didn't seem too concerned, I could only conclude that Benny wasn't the reliable old soul I'd pegged him to be. Maybe seeing friends had made him forget all about actually driving in the parade. But would he have left his beloved Impala all alone for someone else to drive? It was strange.

I made my way over to the starting line to get a few pictures of the floats out in the bright sunlight and before the wear and tear of driving down the road started to wilt their petals. I could hear the low hum of the motors under each float. Christy was standing next to her giant pony also taking photos. I walked over to her.

"The pony looks anxious to trot out," I said.

She nodded as she beamed up at the float. "They've been idling in formation for a good thirty minutes. The drivers are getting anxious too. Sylvia had to step in for Benny. I think she was delaying the start hoping he'd show up."

"Yes, about that. Benny doesn't strike me as irresponsible."

"He's not but frankly between you and me, Sylvia was driving him too hard this week. Benny, fetch me this. Benny, don't dawdle, I need supplies. Benny, the garbage cans are full."

"Do you think he disappeared on purpose to throw a wrench into her plans?" I was back to digging out some juicy, scandalous tidbits, even though they weren't all that juicy or scandalous.

Christy shrugged. "That would be my guess." The mayor's

car started to roll along the white line, the line that guided the drivers who were dealing with some major blind spot issues in their dark boxes. "Looks like we're finally moving. I've got to climb on the float."

"Good luck in the contest," I called.

I headed back toward the sidewalk hoping I could find a place to tuck myself in so I could watch the pony prance along the route. After all, I helped make him. I wanted the float to win first prize. Guess I'd never lost my competitive edge.

CHAPTER 18

I'd squeezed between a man holding a little boy on his shoulders and an older woman clutching her nervous little dog. Considering I was late to the sidewalk, my placement gave me a pretty good view of the grandstand across the street. The city council members had clipboards on their laps to judge the floats. They all looked happy to be there. Judging a parade was probably far more fun than holding a town hall meeting or doing paperwork to keep the city running.

The mayor got mostly cheers and a few intermittent boos. The boo-ers were immediately scolded by one of the council members who stepped up to the microphone to remind people to be respectful to all parade participants. The moment had finally come for the great dragon to make his parade debut. I had expected the float to be a little closer on the tails of the mayor, but there was a large gap. The crowd standing on the sidewalk leaned out and hopped up on toes to get a good view of the dragon. I hated to admit but it was a good float, quite possibly better than the pony.

The dragon float moved forward. Three miles per hour was a

very slow speed. It finally made its way past the starting point and around the slight curve that would take it straight past the grandstand. The judges all looked on with great interest as the big dragon, wings flapping in the wind and big head bobbing from the ride, made its way toward them. Literally toward them.

It took me a second to realize that the nose of the float, the place where I expected the nose of the Impala to be, was not staying on course. The white line disappeared off to the side as the dragon headed toward the grandstand.

At first there were laughs, even amongst the judges. People thought it was all part of the parade, the unruly dragon flying off on his own. But I knew better. And so did the float team members who were sitting both on the float and walking beside it. One of the volunteers started yelling. "Turn right. Hard right! You've lost the line."

But the dragon and the driver weren't paying attention. Then the speed picked up a little, not much, thank goodness. Still, even at five or ten miles per hour there was nothing anyone could do except start jumping out of the way of the runaway float. When it became frighteningly apparent that something was terribly wrong, faces changed and people started fleeing the grandstand. One of the women made it off just in time as the massive dragon head, flames and all, torpedoed right through the banners across the grandstand. Slowly, the force of the car and the weight of the float tipped the grandstand over. The whole moving disaster finally stopped when the float got stuck on the fallen grandstand.

Some people ran away from the float, worried apparently that it might start up again and take out more stands and people. I elbowed my way through the stunned spectators. Brandy was racing toward the accident scene, looking horrified and shocked. Some of the other volunteers followed behind her but seemed more apprehensive about approaching the float, almost as if they considered it a real dragon that might at any moment spin around and shoot fire at them.

I searched around for Benny, but there was no sign of him. None of it made sense, and now his precious Impala had been driven into the grandstand. Several volunteers helped Brandy open the large flap at the back that allowed a car to enter. She disappeared inside. I moved as close as I could get. The area filled with curious spectators, all trying to get a look at the disaster. Whistles had to be blown to get the rest of the parade to stop. The high school band nearly marched right into the entire crowd of spectators. The drum major was red in the face from blowing his whistle to get the attention of the members at the back whose views were blocked by large instruments. There was a small pile up and a few trombones and drums banged into others, but they eventually figured out that the parade had come to a halt.

"This has to be a record for the world's shortest parade," a teenager next to me chortled. His friend laughed. "But it's the most awesome one ever. Did you see that dragon? People were flying off the grandstand." A bit of an exaggeration but I had no doubt that was the version their friends were going to hear.

I managed to get myself a little closer to the dragon. Brandy came out from beneath the open flap. She looked frightened and had her hand to her chest. "Someone call an ambulance." I heard her say over the noise.

It was time for this reporter to grow some sharp elbows. I made my way through the crush of people. The phrase 'call an ambulance' only had people more curious. They moved in on the spectacle enough to make me feel a little panicked. Everyone pushed forward. I found a path to the side that was open and squirted through. I emerged where all the metal chairs had been placed for VIPs.

Some people had taken to standing on the chairs to get a better view of what was happening. I dashed through the array of chairs, ducked under the broken edge of the grandstand and circled around the big dragon's head. Its ears and flames had broken off, and its long neck was tangled in the debris. I skirted down the side of the float and ran into a serious looking volunteer.

"No one is allowed over here. We're trying to clear the area."

I glanced back at the crush of lookie-loos. They hadn't made much headway in getting the crowd back. An ambulance would have no chance of reaching the site. "See if you can find the microphone. It might still be working, then you can make an announcement to clear the area," I suggested.

He was hesitant at first but then saw the size of the crowd descending on the dragon float and rushed away to find the microphone. I reached Brandy. Another volunteer was holding her hand.

"I don't know what's wrong," Brandy sobbed. "I think she just fainted. We need to get that ambulance here soon."

I slipped into the float and pulled out my phone flashlight. I could see Sylvia's head resting against the window as I came up from the rear. I opened the door carefully. An extremely limp Sylvia fell towards the door. I helped her back against the seat, then reached across to turn off the ignition. That was when I noticed her eyes were half open... and lifeless. I stuck my phone in front of her nose and mouth but there was no condensation from breath. It looked to me as if the ambulance wasn't going to help. There was no sign of trauma. Sylvia looked like a woman who took care of herself. How could she have just keeled over behind the wheel of a car?

The impact did a great deal of damage to the grandstand and the float, but the whole thing happened in almost comically slow motion. Was it the accident? There was no sign of bruising on the driver or damage inside the car. It just didn't seem possible that she died from the impact.

A concerned looking volunteer peered into the dark cavity beneath the float. His eyes rounded. "Is she all right? Has Ms. Franco come to?" he asked.

"I'm afraid not. Send the paramedics the moment they arrive," I said.

The young man left. Brandy poked her head in next. "Oh, *you're* in here. Is Sylvia all right? Is she conscious?" Her voice wavered.

"We'll need to wait for the medics." It was not my place to announce that Sylvia was dead. I pulled out my phone. It was time to call Jackson to let him know the parade ended before it started, and there was a dead woman driving a dragon.

CHAPTER 19

The police had been conveniently parked near the parade route in case there was a problem. I doubted they expected the chaos that had erupted when the dragon rolled into the grandstand. The paramedics had been needed after all for a sprained ankle, a congresswoman's heel caught on the steps as she fled the stands. A small fight also broke out when the curious spectators grew too pushy and elbows started jabbing noses. I was thankful that the officers were able to clear the entire area without any other incidents.

I was also thankful to see the tall hunk of man I called honey and also Detective Jackson. He was shaking his head as he entered the float. He had to practically walk on his knees. "How do you do it, Miss Taylor? Parades aren't generally known for dead people but then you were here, so I guess it was a given."

Jackson pulled out his flashlight and shined it on Sylvia's face and arms. "That red mottled skin coloring is something we see with carbon monoxide poisoning. I don't see any signs of trauma." He swept the flashlight all around the inside of the box. "Looks pretty solid. I've never been inside one of these before.

Where does the exhaust leave? And how on earth do they see what's going on outside?"

"I actually know the answers to both those questions." I walked to the front of the car and pointed out the peephole, a slim rectangle at the front of the base. Flower petals were blocking a lot of the opening.

Jackson peered through it. "*That* is a limited view."

"They can see the white line. That's what they follow to stay on course and away from crowds and grandstands. I noticed that Sylvia wasn't following the line. By the way, she wasn't supposed to be driving the car. Benny," I said to myself.

"What about Benny?" Jackson asked.

"He's the guy who was supposed to be driving the float. This is his Impala."

Jackson's flashlight beam reflected off the cherry red paint. "It's pretty sweet. Is Benny Sylvia's husband?"

"No, he's a custodian, a handyman for the event. Nice guy but he disappeared just before the floats were supposed to line up. Sylvia, who seemed to have been somewhat of a micromanager, decided she would drive the float to the starting point. Her dragon was first in line."

"Hold all that stuff you have for when we get out of here. I'm getting a crick in my back from stooping over. How does the exhaust get out of this coffin?"

"Gosh, you're right. It really is like a big coffin. Especially with a corpse in it." I shivered once. "It's starting to get to me."

"You can go. The coroner will be here soon I'm going to see if we can push the car out from this mess. But first—the exhaust."

"Right." I walked to the back of the float. "Within the larger flap that allowed the car to roll inside there's a small, far less visible flap that is left open for ventilation." We stepped outside and pulled down the larger flap we'd opened to allow medical personnel to reach the victim. "Hmm, let me see where it is on this float. I was inside the giant pony." I waved back toward the big smiling pony, his mane fluttering in the wind as he anxiously waited for show time. It would never come. I felt around in the soft petals for the opening, a small hole that was used to lift the invisible flap up. "I don't know why it's not already open. There's a hole somewhere—" Just as I felt around, my fingers grazed something that wasn't flower petals. I pulled the fabric free. It was one of Christy's brown and white checked aprons.

"There's the pony again," Jackson noted.

"Yes, it belongs to the woman in charge of the pony float. It was jammed in the hole, and the vent flap was never opened."

Jackson pulled some of the petals free, uncovering a few strips of duct tape. "Looks like it was sealed shut while the victim was sitting inside the car. The apron was added to make sure none of the exhaust escaped."

I placed my hand on his arm. "Jackson, the floats were sitting at the starting line idling for more than thirty minutes. Do you think—"

"Do I think someone murdered her? Sure looks that way." Jackson looked past my head. "There's the coroner's team. They'll give us a better idea about cause of death, but I'm fairly certain we already know. The question is—who wanted to kill—" He pulled out his notebook. "Sylvia Franco?"

I sighed. "I've got a little insight on that too."

"Why am I not surprised? I've got to talk to the coroner. You can fill me in on details later." He winked at me and walked off toward the coroner's van as it pulled slowly up to the site.

I decided to use the time to do a little exploring in the warehouse. Most everyone had gone home after the police ordered the area cleared. I assumed that meant the warehouse was empty. Snooping was much easier when no one else was around.

The doors were unlocked, which was both good and bad. I

could get inside, but it meant that there might still be people wandering about. I stepped into the building. It was much bigger without the floats. A loud echo followed the clang of the door as I shut it behind me. The overhead fluorescent lights were still on. The cavernous space was a total mess, which was to be expected considering the activity that had gone on inside the warehouse. Just as I concluded that the building was empty, a noise startled me. The echo in the large building made it sound louder and scarier than it was. When I listened for it again, it sounded like someone was rattling a door.

"Someone, let me out," the voice sounded frazzled and distressed, weak even.

The echo made it harder, but I was able to discern the direction the voice came from. I headed across the building to the supply closet. I'd followed Marilyn to the closet when I was helping with the pony float.

I reached the door. It rattled again. "Please," the voice said. I recognized it.

"Benny?" I asked. "Is that you?"

"Who's there? Oh, thank goodness. I've been in here for hours. The door is locked."

I grabbed the knob and turned it. It was locked from the outside. "It's Sunni Taylor, the reporter with the *Junction Times*. I need a key. Do you know where I can find one?"

"Unfortunately, I have mine on my tool belt, but Sylvia has another master set. Ask her for a key."

I didn't want to break the news through a locked door. His voice was so hoarse, he was not in a state to receive shocking news. "I'll be right back. Just sit tight."

He chuckled so quietly it made me sad. "I have no choice in the matter."

I raced through the maze of debris on the floor to the center of the building where Sylvia's desk and manager station had been set up. Her phone was still sitting in the same place she'd left it when she realized her pantsuit didn't have pockets. I got lucky. The key ring, one with at least a dozen keys, was sitting in the top drawer of the desk. I hurried back to the supply closet.

"Bear with me, Benny, I've got a few to try."

"The key has a round top. That should narrow it down."

"Right." There were only three keys with round tops. The second one fit. I turned the knob, and a very exhausted man met me on the other side. There were beads of sweat on his forehead. His shirt was wet.

"Let's get you out of here. Let me see if I can find you some water."

"No, I'm fine." He pointed toward a shelf where two empty water bottles sat next to some granola bar wrappers. "Guess if you're going to get locked in somewhere, make sure it's a stocked supply closet."

"Glad to see you kept your sense of humor through all this. What happened?"

Benny pulled a rag from his pocket and wiped his forehead. "I don't know. Sylvia texted that she needed some floral wire from the supply closet." He pulled the small roll of wire from his pocket. "I raced to the closet to grab the wire and the door slammed shut. I heard the key turn."

"Someone locked you inside on purpose." As I stated the obvious, Benny lifted his head up and confusion crossed his freshly wiped brow.

"Why don't I hear the bands and music? Did the parade end early? Who drove the dragon float? My Impala," he said, suddenly remembering his cherry red baby was out on the parade route without him.

"Benny, you still look drained, and there was a limited supply of oxygen in that closet. Let's get you to a chair. There are a few things I need to tell you, and you're going to want to be seated."

CHAPTER 20

*A*fter I unloaded the entire saga on poor Benny he kept shaking his head and saying 'how could all that have happened while I was locked in a closet?' He was further disappointed when he was told that his beautiful vintage car would have to be impounded temporarily as evidence. At least it had gotten through the crash without a scratch. The same could not be said for Sylvia Franco. The coroner's preliminary examination at the site confirmed Jackson's suspicions. She'd died of carbon monoxide poisoning. While she was relatively young and fit, the coroner suspected some underlying health condition like a bad heart had hastened the death.

Since Christy's apron had been found stuck in the hole that would have given at least some place for the poisonous gas to escape, Jackson called her back to the site. She arrived with a rather 'deer in headlights' look about her. The entire day had been a shock to everyone, but being called back to the parade by the police would put anyone on edge. Especially if you had something to do with the murder.

Christy's furrowed brow and tight lips loosened when she was

approached by Jackson. I'd seen it before, an entire transformation of demeanor, a quick hair fix and even a brief cheek pinch
for color when a woman was about to be questioned by Detective
Brady Jackson. Christy was no different, which made me think
maybe she had nothing to do with the murder. Yes, he was extra-
ordinarily good looking, but if you thought you were about to be
arrested for murder, color in your cheeks just wouldn't be all that
important.

Jackson never minded when I stuck inconspicuously around
for interviews. He'd been so busy with the coroner and evidence
team, I hadn't had a chance to debrief him on everything.
However, I had let him know there was an ongoing rivalry
between Christy Jacobs and Sylvia Franco. That made the need
to talk to Christy even more urgent.

Christy coyly tucked a strand of hair behind her ear. "What's
this all about, Detective Jackson? I had nothing to do with the
dragon float. When the parade started, I was sitting on the big
pony three floats back."

Jackson nodded. He flipped open his notebook. "I assume
you were in the float area while you waited for the parade to
start."

"Yes, we all were. There were a lot of people milling about
the area."

Jackson had the apron in a bag. He lifted it to give her a good
view of the contents. Her reaction was shock. "That's one of my
aprons," she admitted readily. "I made them for my volunteers."

Jackson wrote something on his notepad. "Any idea how it
got jammed into the vent hole on the back of the dragon float?"

She pressed a hand to her chest. "What? How on earth did it
get there? You certainly don't think I put it there? I don't understand. Was this an accident or not?"

Jackson scribbled something down. I could only assume it was
about her reaction. She seemed genuinely befuddled.

"It appears to have been foul play. Your apron was the first major evidence to point us in that direction. It was jammed into the hole that is used to lift open the ventilation flap."

Her face blanched. "Foul play? Murder?" she said on a breath. "I guess it's not all that surprising."

Naturally, it was a statement that caused Jackson's face to pop up. "Why do you say that?"

Christy did a flirty little head toss to once again push her hair off her face. She had his full attention, and she was smitten. Couldn't blame her. So was I.

"First of all, I had those aprons hanging from a hook on the wall near the float assembly area. Anyone could have grabbed one. I made several extras. I'm not surprised because Sylvia had a lot of enemies."

"I understand the two of you were not friends," Jackson tossed out the passively leading statement.

Christy boldly lifted her chin. "I'm not afraid to admit that I despised Sylvia and she despised me. What started out as some competition between our two girls on the cheerleading squad turned into an all out war. It got ugly and we never apologized to each other. Everyone who worked on the float team with me can tell you that she harassed me daily. She also fired Arthur Andrews off of the Founders' Day Committee because he was dating me."

Jackson jotted down some notes. "Arthur Andrews? The same Andrews who used to be on the city council?"

"Yes, that's him. Sylvia took revenge on him because we were seeing each other. Arthur is just another name on Sylvia's enemy list. Not that Arthur had anything to do with it," she added briskly. "Arthur wasn't even at the parade. You might talk to Sylvia's ex-husband," she suggested in an obvious attempt to divert the discussion away from Arthur.

Jackson flipped through his notebook. "Ernie Franco?" he asked.

"Yes, that's him. They had a bitter divorce."

"We just sent some officers to his house to break the news. They have children?" he asked.

For the first time since she'd arrived, Christy actually looked upset about what had happened. After all, enemy or not, a young woman died today. "Two. Poor things. They did dote on their mother. She did everything for them." Her moment of grief was short-lived. "Sylvia kept trying to get the kids to dislike their father. She tried to turn them against him. Ernie was beside himself about it. They're in a big custody battle."

Jackson wrote down all the information. I read his expression. He wasn't going to call her in for a formal interrogation. At least not yet. If Christy was the killer, she was playing it pretty darn cool.

"Anyone else I should add to this list?" he asked.

"Like I said, she had a lot of enemies. She was yelling at her float team throughout the week. Several people switched teams just to get away from her. It would be easier if you asked the question, who liked Sylvia Franco? That would be a much shorter list."

Jackson flipped shut his notebook. "Thanks for your help. We'll be keeping the apron for evidence."

She waved it off. "Like I said, I have extras. You can keep it for as long as you like."

"Did everyone on your team have one of these?" he asked before dismissing her.

"Yes." She glanced at me as I pretended to take photos of the wreckage. "Even that reporter has one. She volunteered to work on our float."

Jackson peered my direction. "Thanks. I'll let you know if we need to talk again."

She nodded. "I'm not a suspect, am I?"

"Not at this time." It was a statement that I'd heard him say many times, and it was never a great comfort to the person receiving it.

Her hand was a little shaky as she once again pushed back some stray strands of hair. "I would never kill her," was all she said before she hurried away.

Jackson strolled over to me. "So you have an apron too?"

"No, I handed it back to Christy's assistant. I'm not really an apron type as you might have noticed."

He smiled. "I guess so."

"What are you thinking? Suspect or not?" I asked.

"She's on the list, but she gave a pretty convincing performance if it was, indeed, a performance."

"Ah ha, that's what I thought too. I'm getting pretty darn good at this murder stuff."

"As much as I hate to admit it, yes, yes you are."

CHAPTER 21

*A*fter getting to the warehouse so early and especially after the stressful day, I was happy to head home. The murder scene was such a chaotic mess what with a smashed up dragon, hundreds of thousands of petals, leaves and seeds and the destroyed grandstand, Jackson and his team had their work cut out.

I turned into my driveway, visions of a hot shower and cold sandwich in my head, when Raine pulled in right behind me. Her tires screeched a little as she threw on the brakes. I glanced in the side view mirror of the jeep and saw that her face was contorted with worry.

I jumped out of the car. "What's wrong? Did something happen?" My heart was pounding before I even reached her.

"Nothing's happened… yet." She took hold of my hand. "I'm glad you're here and all right. I was practicing with some tarot cards. I thought I'd just put your name out there as my imaginary client and…" She shook her head and swallowed hard. "I need a glass of water. I was so scared all the way over here. Why didn't you answer my text?"

I pulled out my phone. "Are you all right?" she'd texted.

"I was driving. My phone was inside my purse. As you can see, I'm fine. Maybe it was a bad reading because I wasn't actually there." It would have been easy enough to wave off a bad reading, except, more than once, Raine's premonitions and card readings had accurately predicted something dire.

Raine was still shaken when she stepped into the kitchen. I hurried to the cupboard for a glass and filled it with cold water.

She took it readily. "Thanks, I'm parched from fright. I was so sure something had happened."

I sat down next to her and hugged her. "As you can see I'm fine. However, there was a big accident and murder at the parade."

Raine took a few more gulps, then lowered the glass and took what I figured was her first decent breath since those darn tarot cards had freaked her out. "I heard the parade was a terrible disaster. That led me to be even more worried. I knew you were at the parade. There was rumor that a woman died." She took a long shuddering breath. I hugged her again.

"I'm sorry I gave you such a fright."

We'd relaxed for a few minutes, both of us returning to a more calm state. My heart was no longer slamming into my rib cage, and an even color was returning to Raine's complexion.

"I think we need some hot tea." I got up to put the kettle on and came face-to-face with a dour looking ghost. I glanced over at Raine, a habit I had whenever Edward appeared and Raine was in the room. I supposed, deep down, I was hoping she'd see Edward like her friend, Dex. He could not only see Edward, but he could see and communicate with any spirit he came across. Fortunately, Dex was not in the business of outing ghosts. He had far too much respect for incorporeal beings. So my huge secret remained just that—a huge secret. As badly as I wanted to let Raine in on it, I'd avoided telling her. It would only complicate things.

If I'd been alone in the kitchen I would have asked my especially gloomy ghost why he looked so grim. I winked at him and carried on with the task of filling the kettle.

"Where's Brady?" Edward asked. The serious edge in his tone made me turn to look at him. Raine was busy scrolling through her phone and didn't notice.

I tossed a shrug his way. The expression he wore bordered on uneasy. It wasn't one I saw often. It was certainly making me uneasy as well.

Edward said nothing more. He drifted across to stare out the front window. I assured myself he was just in a strange mood. Wouldn't be the first time.

Raine put down her phone. "Where's Jackson?" It wasn't a 'hey, where's the hunky boyfriend' question. It had a worried edge, much like Edward's.

I laughed lightly. "He's at work. Dead woman at the parade, remember? It was a big mess involving an out of control dragon and some flying city council members." I ended the farcical statement with another light laugh. Raine wasn't amused or the least bit curious about the flying council members.

The tea kettle startled all of us, even Edward. That was unusual in itself, but he was beginning to fidget with the ends of his waistcoat. His gaze was dark with concern. "Will Brady be here soon?" Edward asked.

I shook my head with as little movement as possible. I poured the water into the tea cups but had to admit even a cup of hot honey lemon tea didn't sound soothing. Raine looked as if the hair was standing up on the back of her neck, and Edward looked like the world's most agitated Englishman.

I placed a cup of tea in front of Raine. She stared down at it as if I'd placed a cup of spiders in front of her.

In the meantime, Edward was only adding to my angst. "He should be here. You should summon him."

Just as he said it, Raine's face popped up. Her eyes were round behind her glasses. "Call Jackson." It was a command. "Call him now."

I didn't even question her. The look on her face, the rigid set of her shoulders had super charged my pulse again. My heart was flopping wildly around in my chest. I grabbed my phone and dialed Jackson. There was some relief from my pounding pulse when he answered.

He sounded harried, winded. "Hey, anything wrong?"

I realized then that I didn't have a true reason for calling. I wasn't about to let him know that both my psychic best friend and intuitive ghost were freaking out about him. My hesitation must have caused him to stop. I no longer heard his footsteps and his breathing slowed.

"Sunni?"

"Yes, uh, I was just wondering how the case was going."

"Someone found where Sylvia's car was parked a few miles from the end of the parade route. I'm almost there. It's just down the block. We found her keys and all her personal belongings in her desk." The beep of a car being unlocked by remote popped through the phone. It was immediately followed by an explosion that was so loud Raine stood up, and I, instinctively, pulled the phone from my ear. The last thing I heard was Jackson groan or growl or possibly curse. I couldn't tell. The phone went dead.

"Jackson, Jackson!" I yelled into the phone.

Edward's expression was so grave as he swept across the room, a sob fell from my lips. He stopped so close to me, I could feel the coolness of his aura surrounding me, enveloping me almost like a hug.

"What was that?" Raine asked. She looked close to tears too. "It sounded like an explosion."

All I could do was nod in response as I quickly redialed Jackson. It went straight to voicemail. My throat went dry with fear.

"I have to go there," I croaked the words out. I covered my face and took some deep breaths to keep myself from breaking into hysterical sobs.

"You can't drive. I'll take you," Raine's voice wavered. "It'll be fine. I just know he'll be fine."

I dropped my hands. "Do you think so? Are you getting a feeling?" I asked. It was amazing how quickly I relied on her sixth sense when I wanted it to be true and correct. "Please tell me you're getting a good feeling, Raine."

She couldn't look at me. "Let me look for my keys."

"Raine?" I pleaded.

She lifted her face. "I'm not getting anything. I'm not sure." Tears filled her eyes.

I looked frantically at Edward. He was also avoiding eye contact. "Is he all right?" I was no longer worried about ghost-protocols. This was too important.

"I don't know," Edward said. "I don't know."

Raine looked perplexed. She stared toward the empty space in the kitchen where I'd thrown my question. She took my hand. "Let's go. I'm sure he'll be fine. He just has to be."

CHAPTER 22

*R*aine was driving at top speed but it still felt like we were moving in slow motion. I had my seatbelt on, but I sat forward, gripping the dash as if that would somehow get us there faster. Everything looked extra vivid as we flew through town; the red and white striped awning on the ice cream shop; the three pigeons who sat on the back of the bus bench as if they were waiting for the five o'clock bus; the elderly woman who took a painstakingly long time to cross the street with her fluffy dog. It was strange, the ridiculous things that occurred to you when your emotions were on overload. I practically dug holes into Raine's dash as we waited for the lady to shuffle across, and I kept thinking that the dog looked the same on both ends. How did she know which end to feed?

Orange cones were set up across most of the road leading to the parade site. I took that as an ominous sign and groaned in agony. My fingers clumsily felt for the window button. I rolled it down to get some fresh air. Nausea was starting to make my head spin.

Raine pulled over to the curb. "I don't think I can get any closer."

A puff of smoke lingered in the air about a mile away. "I'll go the rest of the way on foot." The car drive was making me anxious and nauseous. I needed the cool air in my face and control over my own speed. I climbed out of the car. I knew that my long legs could carry me faster than most people.

"Go on, I'll never keep up with you," Raine said. "I'll be right behind and, Sunni—" She raced over and hugged me. "It'll be fine," she whispered in my ear. "I just know it will."

The second she released me, I took off at an all out sprint toward the cloud of smoke. It smelled acidic and chemical, not like the comforting smell of wood burning in a hearth.

"Hey, no one is allowed through there," an officer yelled from the far corner as I passed an intersection. I ignored him and continued at full speed. If I'd been participating in a track race, the ribbon would have been mine.

I was making good progress, but my feet and heart and pounding pulse froze in time at the sight of the bomb squad vehicle, a big, black monster that looked more tank than truck.

I glanced around frantically for someone I knew, for the face that I longed to see. An ambulance was parked fifty yards away from the bomb squad vehicle. The rear door was open and a medic stood in the opening tending to someone.

"Miss, you can't be here," someone said from behind. It was a familiar young officer. He knew me as soon as I turned around. "Miss Taylor." He looked toward the ambulance, and his expression made my knees weak. He reached for me. "Detective Jackson is in the ambulance."

I gripped his arm to keep upright. "Is he—" I didn't know how to finish the sentence. I didn't like any of the words that came to mind.

"He's fine. Just a little shaken and a few cuts."

It took me a second to absorb his words through the haze of terror clouding my head. Once the words came through loud and clear, a sob of relief burst from my lips. I took off, once again, at a full run toward the ambulance. A few feet before I reached the rear door the medic stepped back. Another sob of relief.

Jackson was sitting in the back of the ambulance with a silver wrapper around his shoulders. He was holding a piece of gauze to a wound on his arm. Two bandages crossed his forehead and one held together a minor cut on his cheek. He looked a little slumped over and out of it, but when he saw me he straightened. The metallic emergency blanket slipped from his shoulders. With a grunt of pain, he stepped out of the ambulance.

I badly want to jump into his arms but I stopped. I hadn't realized how hard I was crying until a hiccup jolted me.

"Sunni," he said quietly and wrapped his arms around me. I pressed my face against his shirt. "I'm sorry. My phone broke—" I was listening to his deep voice as it moved haltingly through his chest. It wasn't straight and strong and confident, the voice I was used to. It had a tremor in it. He was shaken. The usually unflappable Detective Jackson was shaken.

It took some doing but I collected myself. I had to pull away from him when the medic insisted he take one more blood pressure reading.

Jackson sat down in the ambulance. "I think this arm fared better than the other. He slowly rolled up his sleeve. That was when I noticed a series of small nicks and abrasions along his entire arm. He winced and the medic apologized over and over as he worked to get the cuff in place.

His reading was fine. "Can I go?" Jackson asked the paramedic.

The medic was a young man who was still in the throes of teenage acne. He looked hesitant about giving an order to a detective. "Uh, I've been told you're supposed to go to the hospital to be checked out."

"I've been checked out." Jackson showed him his arm again. "What you see is it. Admittedly, my ears are ringing, and something tells me I'll be startling at the sound of a car backfiring for some time but I'm fine."

The medic nodded as if he agreed that Jackson probably didn't need to go. At the same time, he insisted he was following orders.

Jackson looked to me to make sure I was on his side. I shook my head. "I think it wouldn't hurt for you to get checked out. What if there was permanent damage to your ears?"

The paramedic flashed me a thank you smile for siding with him. "I'll be right back," he said. "I've got to call the hospital to let them know."

I moved closer and took his hand. There were tiny nicks all over his knuckles. "What happened? I've never been so scared in my life, and considering some of the predicaments I've gotten into, that's saying a lot."

"It sure is." He squeezed my hand tighter. "Your phone call saved my life, Bluebird. I was on my way to Sylvia's car. I stopped a good fifty yards from the vehicle. You know how it's just habit to click the remote long before you reach the vehicle. I pushed the unlock button. Seconds later, the car exploded. If I hadn't stopped to talk to you, I would have been much closer to that car. Then I wouldn't be sitting here with just a bunch of cuts and bruises. Heck, I wouldn't be sitting here at all."

His words sent a wave of dizziness through me. I swayed on my feet. "Sit here, Sunni. You look pale." I sat next to him and the lightheadedness faded. He'd come so close to dying.

"Sunni!" Raine called from behind the police line. An officer was holding out his arm to block her from entering the scene.

"It was Raine," I blurted. The last hour had been such a

nightmarish blur. It was all coming back to me. "Raine told me to call you. She was frantic and insisted I call you, but she gave me no reason. And Edward"—I put my hand to my chest—"Edward knew something was wrong."

"Officer Evans, it's all right. Let her through," Jackson called.

The officer stepped aside. Raine pushed through. She ran to us. "Jackson, thank goodness." She leaned over and hugged him.

"I hear I have you to thank for still being alive," he said.

Raine blinked at him in confusion. "I don't understand."

"Jackson stopped to answer my call. He unlocked the car from where he was standing and it exploded."

Raine covered her mouth and muffled a sob.

"You and that wonderful sixth sense, Raine." I stood up and we hugged. "You can add lifesaving psychic to your resume."

I turned to Jackson. "So, if Sylvia's car blew up—"

Jackson nodded. "I assume that they had a backup plan in case the carbon monoxide didn't work. Someone really wanted that woman dead."

CHAPTER 23

*I*t was close to nine o'clock at night by the time the doctors released Jackson. They checked for internal damage and concussion and took time to inspect each cut for shrapnel or any debris that might have flown his direction during the explosion. A few splinters were removed here and there, but, for the most part, his cuts were clean. He had a massive bruise on his right hip where he landed after instinctively jumping as far away from the explosion as possible. That was when his phone flew out of his hand and smacked the ground. The department had sent him a new phone before he even left the emergency room. There was also a message from the higher-ups that he was on paid leave for five days. Most people would be relieved to hear it, but Jackson was miffed. He wanted to get right to work to find the maniac who planted the bomb.

I was making him his favorite late night snack—tomato soup and a grilled cheese sandwich. He'd taken two aspirin for headache, a lingering effect the doctor warned might last a few days. Along with the ringing in his ears.

Edward kept circling the table where Jackson sat, apparently making sure he was all right. Jackson finally looked up from his glass of tea. "Gramps, if you're wondering whether I've joined you in your strange little world, I'm sorry to tell you that I'm still flesh and blood. Although, I have a little less of both of those right now."

"It is quite apparent that you are still flesh and blood. And I see your character is still the same, aggravating and arrogant."

"Me?" Jackson laughed, then winced and pressed his hand to his bruised side.

"What's happening?" Edward couldn't hide the worry in his voice. He looked my direction. "Is he all right? Does he have some kind of internal complaint? I once knew a man who was thrown from his horse. He stood up, brushed himself off and climbed right back on. Five hours later, he dropped dead in the middle of the general store. Just like that."

"We have machines that help doctors make sure there is no hidden injury or internal complaint," I explained. "Jackson is just sore from landing forcefully on a hard sidewalk. I imagine you'll be feeling that bruise for a week."

"Machines that can see inside a human?" Edward asked. There was a glint of awe in his blue eyes. "It's astounding what men can do."

"And women," I reminded him curtly. I lifted the grilled cheese off the pan. It wasn't one of Emily's decadent, gooey masterpieces but it would do. I poured the tomato soup into a bowl and carried the meal to the table.

For the third time, I gazed at Jackson through teary eyes. How easily I could have lost him.

He looked up from his soup when he heard my sniffle. He put down the spoon and looked at me. "It's all right, Bluebird. You're not getting rid of me that easily."

I grabbed a napkin and blotted my eyes. "Don't tease, Jax. I aged ten years this afternoon. I'm afraid to look in the mirror for fear that a haggard old woman will be staring back at me."

Jackson squinted at me. "Actually, I do see a few more lines."

I balled up the napkin and threw it at him.

He picked up his spoon. "Now you know how I feel every time you *cross the line* in an investigation."

"I never cross the line," I insisted. "I merely scoot around it."

"It's a dangerous job you have," Edward said. "You should switch to something altogether more suitable to the Beckett bloodline."

Jackson finished a bite of sandwich. "More suitable? What did men of your snooty breeding do anyhow? Other than stealing another man's wife and all that scandalous stuff, Mr. Beckett and his blue bloodline."

"Why, we—we rode horses, went on fox hunts, spent good weather days in the country shooting pheasant and then there were the various social gatherings—"

Jackson's laugh interrupted Edward's list, which was probably for the best. "You're right. I'll just ride horses, do a little bird hunting and show up at balls in my tails and top hat. Silly me wasting all this time working on the police force when I could be taking tea with all the other snobs in town. Why didn't I think of that before?" He tapped the table. "That's right. It's because none of those delightful activities pay actual money. Since I wasn't to the manor born, as they say—though, I'm not sure who *they* is except I'm sure they're just as snooty as you." Jackson was definitely feeling himself again. After the terrible incident he looked rattled, both physically and mentally. It took him only a few hours to recuperate and return to his usual confident self.

"I see the explosion didn't knock that ridiculous sense of humor out of you," Edward sniped back. Once again, it was time for an intermediary to step in.

"All right. First of all, Mr. Beckett, with your fox hunting and social gatherings, this afternoon you were in the most fretful state I'd ever seen you in and all because you sensed Jackson was in danger. And you were right. It shows, one—that you care about him, and two—that you two are connected both by genes and something else, something I can't explain." Jackson would have spoken up to protest if he hadn't just stuffed his mouth with grilled cheese. "And you, Mr. Jackson," I said pointedly, "you have been worried nonstop about how opening an inn was going to negatively affect Edward's existence. No point in denying it, even after you swallow, because you know it's true."

He swallowed and jumped into it anyhow. "That was selfishness on my part. I was projecting. At least that's what I think they call it. Yes, I thought the old man here was going to be put out by a load of guests staying at the inn, but I also worried how it would affect me."

It was the first time he'd said anything like it. "I don't understand," I said, quietly confused.

"Running an inn was going to be a full time job. You weren't going to have much free time. I worried that between my long hours and yours, we wouldn't have time for each other. Sorry, I guess today's brush with death made me think I should put all my cards on the table."

Edward, naturally, glanced at the table to look for the actual cards. I laughed. The idiom thing would never get old.

"I think it's sweet that you were worried about not spending enough time with me, Jax. That played into my decision too."

Edward cleared his throat loudly, a sound that was so forced it reminded me of car tires on gravel. "Then there is the matter of... well... of me."

"The center of the universe speaks," Jackson teased.

"Yes, glad we agree on that. What exactly are you speaking of when you say universe?"

Jackson looked back over his shoulder. He was moving way

slower than usual. "For those of us still alive, it means the planets, the stars and everything around us. For you, it means this house and the front stoop."

I reached my foot across and tapped Jackson's toes telling him to stop. Their banter usually ended with Edward's feelings being hurt. Then I was stuck with a gloomy ghost dragging around the house looking about as sad as a kid who dropped his ice cream cone.

Jackson took the subtle cue and gladly returned his focus to his soup and sandwich.

"Guys," I said, "can't believe I'm saying this, but I need your opinions on something."

Jackson's brows rose. "You need *his* opinion?"

"Certainly she does. She obviously sees that you make poor choices." Edward moved closer, anxious to give his opinion. (Not that he ever needed to be asked.)

"What poor choices?" Jackson asked.

I sighed loudly. It was starting again.

"Well, which one of us is sitting in this kitchen with silly patches all over his face and arms?" Edward asked.

"They're bandages, not patches. And which of us sitting in this kitchen is dead? Dead, I might add, because of some majorly poor decisions."

Edward had no good response because it was true. His image spun toward me, almost like a tornado with bits and molecules spinning around a vortex, namely his Hessian boots. "What do you need my venerated opinion on?" That gave Jackson another chuckle, but it seemed he was done with the back and forth. What he needed was to finish his meal and go to bed.

I took a deep breath. "All right, here goes."

My prelude caused Jackson to look up from his sandwich. "Sounds important."

I nodded. "It is. I was thinking of letting Raine in on our

little, actually, our huge, secret."

Both men blinked at me with their big, attractive eyes. They had no idea what secret I was referring to.

I took another breath. "Well, that didn't go the way I thought. I'm thinking of letting Raine know that Edward exists."

"Of course I exist. I'm standing right here," Edward drawled.

Jackson glanced pointedly at his boots as they hovered a good three inches above the floor. "That's a matter of opinion. Speaking of opinions—not sure that's a good idea. The more people who know, the more chances of our secret getting out. And ghosts are kind of her thing. It would be extra hard for her to keep it under wraps."

"Yes, I agree with that, but I'd swear her to secrecy first."

"Once again, you two are speaking gibberish. How are ghosts her *thing*?" His face smoothed. "Oh, I see. You're worried that she'll fall in love with me."

Jackson laughed and grabbed his side.

"Oh good, I hope that hurt," Edward added.

"No, she won't fall in love with you. At least that's not where this conversation was going, but now it's getting late and the day has been so stressful and the two of you together behaving like siblings—anyhow, Raine saved your life today. I just think this is something that she would want to know. She has sensed a presence in the house all along. I can make her happy by letting her know her sixth sense is working. It certainly worked today."

"I would rather not have to communicate with that silly woman, but if it's what you want," Edward said, "I can allow her to see and hear me."

"Thank you, Edward." I looked at Jackson for his approval.

He shook his head. "I'm not saying no. Just give it a lot of thought first. However, I do appreciate what she did today, and when I'm feeling better, I'm going to let her know that I owe her… big time."

CHAPTER 24

*J*ackson stayed at my house and decided he was too sore to get out of bed. I brought him eggs and toast. His ears were still ringing, but his headache had softened to a dull ache. Edward never entered my personal space area in the house, so I warned Jackson if he didn't want to get into an annoying argument with Edward, he should just stay in bed. He had no problem with that. I let him know I was going out to run some errands and buy him his favorite ice cream—chocolate peanut butter—and that I'd be back later. I had every intention of running the errands and buying the ice cream, but first, I decided a trip to the warehouse might prove fruitful. After all, I still had a lead story to write. It just wasn't going to be the flowery pony and dragon story I was planning. Somewhere in our fair town was a monster who wanted Sylvia Franco dead so badly, they had a backup method in case the first one failed. The second method was far more sinister, took way more planning and could have killed more people than the intended victim. As Jackson had pointed out to me, if the parade had gone on as planned and the

murder hadn't led to the police clearing the area, a lot of innocent bystanders could have been harmed by the blast. Jackson
had also noted that setting a bomb so that it exploded when
someone unlocked the car took a lot of expertise. The person
who wanted Sylvia dead wasn't just some angry float competitor.
They had to know how to build and detonate a device. That took
a great deal of skill and experience. He was sure they'd have
someone in custody today because the list would be narrow. Not
many people in Firefly, let alone people who just happened to
hate Sylvia Franco, had that particular set of skills.

Not surprisingly, there were a few cars parked in the lot in
front of the warehouse. Now that the crime scene search was
over, it gave the volunteers a chance to clean up. The warehouse
had been left in a state of total chaos. I was fairly certain the
small red car sitting just east of the big sliding door belonged to
Sylvia's assistant, Brandy. I hoped it did so I could talk to her
more. Maybe she knew if any of Sylvia's enemies had bomb
making skills. Then, it occurred to me, the area had been cleared
well in advance of the bomb exploding. It was highly likely that
Brandy and the other parade workers didn't know about the
second attack on Sylvia's life. Was I at liberty to say something? I
decided not to mention it unless she did, then I'd have every right
to pry further.

A few volunteers were scattered throughout the building,
pushing brooms around and filling trash cans with debris. There
was no sign of Benny. Maybe he'd had enough of the whole
thing.

Brandy was sitting at the desk where Sylvia had placed her
project manager station. She was holding a handkerchief in one
hand while stacking paperwork with the other.

"Brandy," I said quietly, not wanting to startle her.

She looked up with puffy eyes and a red nose. "It's you. I'm
afraid I'm not much company for an interview this morning. As

you can see, I'm cleaning up." She stopped and blew her nose. "It really hit me hard when I walked in here and saw the empty desk. I was so used to seeing Sylvia standing here, shouting orders, sending off texts and rummaging through purchase orders. I just can't believe she's gone." She put her hands to her face.

I patted her shoulder. "It's a big shock. I can only imagine."

She lowered her hands and peered up at me. "Did they find who did it? I heard that someone sealed shut the exhaust flap." She shuddered. "What a horrible way to die."

Not nearly as horrible as being blown to bits by a bomb. This time I shuddered as my mind crept back to that dark corner where the thought I was trying to bury kept raising its ugly head. *I could have lost him. Just a few more yards and I would have lost him forever.*

"Carbon monoxide is such an unexpected way to go. No, they haven't found the killer."

Her hand flew to her mouth. "That word, it frightens me. I mean, you hear it on television and in the movies, but never in your day-to-day life, especially not in reference to a good friend."

"Was she a good friend?" It was probably an ill-timed question, but I was curious to hear what Brandy really thought of Sylvia. The interactions I'd witnessed were not something I'd label as friendly. Vicious was a more accurate word.

Brandy's round cheeks bunched up. "She was. I mean Sylvia could be a little harsh and bossy but then you don't get to where she was without beating in a few heads. I've been working as her assistant for five years. There were good times and bad, but I enjoyed my work." She teared up again. "I don't know what I'll do now." She once again pushed her hands to her mouth. "How awful that sounds. Here, poor Sylvia is dead, and I'm worried about my next job."

"It's perfectly acceptable to think of yourself at this time. You've gone through quite a shock."

Brandy lowered the lid on the laptop sitting on the desk. She absently ran the dust cloth over it. "I just don't understand how this happened."

"Are you friends with Sylvia's husband? I was just wondering how he's doing." I was also wondering just how nasty the divorce got, but I didn't want to put words in her head.

Brandy lowered her head and shook it. "I'm sure Ernie is devastated and the kids..." Her voice broke. "Those poor kids." Again her hands covered her face. This time her shoulders shook. I gave her a minute to collect herself.

"I understand they were divorced." I'd lost my thread of questioning to her moment of grief.

She blew her nose and pushed the tissue into her pocket, resolutely, as if telling herself, enough was enough, get a grip. "Yes, and it was a terribly bitter divorce." She'd shaken off her despair and seemed anxious to tell someone what she knew about Ernie, the ex. "They fought over everything. The custody battle is ongoing. I suppose now it'll be resolved. Ernie is all the kids have now." She took a steadying breath. "Sylvia tried so hard to get the kids to dislike their father. She told them all kinds of lies about him. I told her it wasn't nice, but she laughed it off and told me I'd never been married so I didn't know anything about it. Ernie was on a few dating sites. Sylvia would troll him, pretend to be some woman who was interested in a date. He didn't really deserve it, but that's how Sylvia was." She gasped and looked up at me. "You don't think Ernie could be the killer, do you? I hadn't thought of that. How awful, then the kids would have no one."

"I'm obviously not the police, but I'm sure they'll find who did it soon enough. What does Ernie do? Just collecting details for my article," I added in quickly, not wanting to start rumors. Brandy seemed ready to start them too.

"Ernie works at the big car dealership off Crimson Grove. He's a salesman. Does pretty well too," she added unnecessarily.

I glanced down at the desk. Brandy had already tidied up the paperwork. I assumed the police had Sylvia's phone, but for some reason, they left the laptop. "I'm surprised the police didn't confiscate Sylvia's computer."

She was puzzled by my statement. "Oh, right." She put her hand on the laptop. "This one's mine. The police did take Sylvia's."

"Brandy"—one of the volunteers had rolled over a dolly with a trash can that was overflowing with debris—"Is Benny coming in?" the woman asked. "The trash cans are getting full."

"He's off today. We'll have to try and dump them ourselves."

The woman grunted something about not getting paid for the job as she pushed the can away.

Brandy rolled her eyes. "They're helpless without leadership. I told Benny to stay home today. Poor man was so shaken about yesterday. Apparently, someone locked him in the supply closet. I have no idea how it happened. I actually think it might just have been an accident. Anyhow, I told him we could manage without him today. It might have been a mistake, but he earned the day off. He worked so hard this week. Sylvia had him running around like a madman with his hair on fire." She giggled at her analogy.

"I guess you're sort of in charge now that Sylvia's—well—you know."

Brandy's face dropped. "I told myself I need to stay strong until we get this job done. We have to have the whole place cleared out and cleaned up by Tuesday. That's when the short term lease runs out."

"I'll let you get back to work then. Thanks for talking to me and again, I'm so sorry about your friend." I'd hoped to sneak around Sylvia's work area but since Brandy had already tidied it up, I thought a trip out to the car dealership on Crimson Grove

127

CHAPTER 25

ow are you feeling?" I texted Jackson. I didn't want
to call him in case he was sleeping. He called back.

"Hey, are you almost home?" he asked.

I smiled to myself. "Why? Do you miss me? Or, let me guess
—you're hungry."

"Both, of course. By the way, got a call from the coroner.
Sylvia Franco did have some heart problems, a deformed aorta or
something like that. He said since she was young and generally fit
and trim, she probably didn't realize she had it. But it meant her
heart was weaker than the average ticker, so the carbon
monoxide did its work quicker."

"Good to know. Anything on the bomb?"

"Forensics is still examining it. Where are you at?"

"In the jeep."

"Yes but where on this fine planet is the jeep? And you know
that was exactly what I meant, so I take it you're out doing your
own investigation."

I didn't answer.

"Your silence says it all. May I remind you we're talking about a killer with a highly sophisticated knowledge of explosives?"

"Trust me, you'll never, ever have to remind me of that. I think I'm still in the aging process from yesterday. I feel like I ran some kind of uphill marathon with a wagon of bricks in tow."

"I'm feeling the same. And I am kind of hungry. I think I'll venture into the kitchen and make myself a piece of toast."

"That's fine but Jax—"

"I know what you're going to say. I'll try to ignore him, but it's not easy. He's like that little mosquito that keeps buzzing in your ear, and as often as you swat at it, it just doesn't go away."

I sighed. "Now I'm feeling much better about the whole toast adventure. Just be nice. If you had seen his expression yesterday when he sensed that you were in trouble, it was actually pretty sweet."

"Yeah, silly old Gramps."

"Don't call him Gramps. You know he hates that."

"You're right. There should be a truce today since he was part of the reason I'm still walking around."

"That's right and don't forget it. I'll see you soon."

The car dealership had long strands of helium balloons tied to every other vehicle in the lot advertising a big sale and low interest rates. Even so, for a Saturday, business was slow. The lot was mostly empty of customers. The sales team huddled on the sidewalk in front of the showroom waiting to swoop down on potential customers.

I sensed there was a game of rock, paper, scissors happening as I stepped onto the lot. And the winner (or loser if they decided I was just a browser) was a woman with thick caramel hair piled up in a bun. She was wearing a t-shirt that read *ask me about our factory rebates*.

"Tired of that jeep?" she asked, motioning toward my beloved vehicle. She stuck out her hand. "I'm Gayle."

I'd considered pretending to be a customer, but I just couldn't stomach a whole sales pitch. I didn't want to raise her hopes that she was about to make a sale. I stuck with the truth.

I pulled out my press pass. "Actually, I'm Sunni Taylor with the *Junction Times*. I was covering the Founders' Day Parade yesterday. I'm sure you heard what happened."

Her mouth turned down. "Terrible tragedy. Ernie's at home with the kids today. They're all just devastated."

"I can only imagine. I was hoping to learn a little bit about him just so I can mention him in the article. So he's a salesman here?" I started with the least prying question. Her answer would let me know whether I'd gotten lucky and found a chatty coworker or unlucky and found a tight-lipped one.

The frown transformed into a gentle smile. "He's won top salesman six months in a row. Everyone loves Ernie. Especially the customers."

I wrote down what she said. "I understand he was no longer married to Sylvia."

Gayle looked around, either to make certain we were alone or to make sure she wasn't missing out on some actual serious customers. Might have been a touch of both.

"The breakup was really hard on Ernie. Not that he wanted to stay with Sylvia. I didn't know her too well, but from what others have told me, she was quite difficult." Her frown retuned. "May she rest in peace, of course."

"Of course. I understand there was a custody battle?"

She shrugged. "That's what I've heard, but it seems like you already know more than me. Maybe I should be asking the questions." She laughed airily, then tossed one out. "Have they found the killer? Are the police suspecting Ernie? It's almost always the spouse, isn't it?" She waved her hand. "They're looking at the wrong person. Ernie was here all day yesterday. We worked the morning shift together. That is until the police showed up with the dreadful news."

"So Ernie was here all morning?" I asked.

"Yup, two of the salespeople were out sick, so it was just Ernie and me on the lot. Wasn't very busy though because everyone was at the parade."

"Yes, I was there. The sidewalks were packed." I decided to leave off the detail about no one getting to see an actual parade. I was sure she could figure that out for herself. It seemed Ernie had a solid alibi, at least for the float sabotaging portion of the crime. But what about the bomb? Did he have an accomplice working the parade? "This might sound like a far out of left field question —but, by any chance, did Ernie have skills in bomb making? Was he possibly in the military?"

Her eyes narrowed. It seemed I'd asked too far out of a question. "You said you're with the paper, right? Almost sounds like you're with the police."

"Nope, just a nosy, curious reporter." I'd found that self-deprecation often worked when I'd crossed the line. Like we were buddies discussing how annoying reporters could be.

"So what Brian was saying this morning must be true." It worked. Now we were such buddies I was expected to know who Brian was and exactly what he'd been saying this morning.

"Brian?" I asked.

"One of the other salespeople. He said that a car exploded somewhere near the parade route. After the crowds had dispersed, thank goodness. But rumor has it a police officer was nearly killed."

It took me a second to respond as the horrid day came back to me. "Uh, I'm not sure about all those details, but yes, apparently a car exploded." I decided not to add anything else.

Oddly enough, after the serious topic, she laughed. "It wasn't Ernie. He can't even fill the coffee maker without messing things up. Least mechanical man I've ever met." Her gaze followed a young, anxious looking couple. "Oops, there are some first time buyers if I've ever seen them. If you don't mind—" She motioned that direction.

"Not at all. Thanks for your time."

As I headed toward the jeep, I realized I'd just mentally scratched a prime suspect off the list.

CHAPTER 26

*A*s I drove back toward Firefly Junction, I noticed Brandy's little red car was no longer parked outside the warehouse. There were two other cars left. The building was huge. With some luck and some expert sneaking about, I would be able to get a look at Sylvia's desk area, the heart of the operation. I wasn't sure there would be anything of note there, but I didn't have too many other places to look or people to interview. I was sure the police would solve this one quickly because of the bomb. There couldn't be too many people in town with bomb making skills, particularly ones who had a vendetta against Sylvia Franco.

I parked the jeep in front of the warehouse yet again. Walking to the front door reminded me about the man who nearly ran down Marilyn and me with our donut boxes. His name was Arthur Andrews, and he certainly was not Sylvia's friend, at least according to Marilyn. Sylvia had removed him from the Founders' Day Committee out of pettiness, again, at least according to Marilyn. Andrew was dating Christy, Sylvia's biggest rival. But would getting kicked off a committee for a social event really push someone to murder?

I walked inside the building. Two volunteers were just finishing cleaning up the restrooms in the warehouse. They must have pulled the short coffee stirrers. I crept quietly over to Sylvia's desk where I would be hidden from view behind a short wall. Not that I needed much cover. The desk had been cleared of everything, paperwork, laptop, office supplies. It seemed my chance to snoop had come and gone.

I pulled open the slim desk drawer just in case something of interest had been forgotten or stored inside. Two broken pencils and an empty roll of tape were the only things left. I slid the drawer shut, but it got stuck halfway. It was an old industrial style desk, so having the drawer stick didn't seem too unusual. I pulled the drawer out, gave it a little jiggle to loosen it up, then shut it again. This time it didn't just get stuck. It sounded as if a sheet of paper ripped.

I glanced across the building to the restrooms. The volunteers had not come out yet. I pulled the drawer all the way out. It got stuck going that direction too but that was to be expected. Otherwise, the drawer would fall out or land in someone's lap every time it was opened too far. I placed the drawer on top of the desk and stooped down to get a look inside. An envelope, now slightly ripped, hung down from tape. Someone had purposely hidden the envelope above the drawer.

My investigator's adrenaline was pumping as I carefully unstuck the tape. I didn't want to cause any more damage to the envelope in case it held crucial evidence. The small rip I'd caused by pushing the drawer in didn't seem to affect the contents. The thickness and dark silhouette through the white envelope told me it contained cash. I peeled back the tape and pulled out five one hundred dollar bills. If this had been a petty cash fund for the committee, it seemed like an odd place to keep it. And it seemed no one, not even Sylvia's loyal assistant, knew its location. It wasn't marked petty cash. Petty cash generally meant small change, dollars, extra bills to be used for coffee runs and such. Hundred dollar bills just didn't fit the *bill*.

As I attempted to slide the bills back into the envelope, once again I hit a snag. This time one of the bills stuck to a small sliver of paper. It had been torn hastily off a full sheet. Someone had written a note in black ink. The writing was barely legible and looked as if it had been written in a rush or in anger. *Last payment. I'm done with blackmail.*

I reread the scribbled note just in case I was reading it wrong. As messy as the writing was, it said exactly what I thought. It wasn't signed, and there was no way of knowing who it'd been written to, but since it was taped inside the desk Sylvia was using to manage the project, it seemed she was the likely person. Was she blackmailing someone? That sure put a new spin on things. Unless the hidden envelope, cold hard cash and shocking note had nothing to do with Sylvia's death, it seemed I was holding some crucial evidence.

I pulled out my phone and dialed Jackson. This time, I woke him. He answered groggily and with a big yawn that he didn't try to mute by covering the phone. "Hey, Bluebird. Where are you at?"

"I'm in a big warehouse. Sorry I woke you."

"Yeah, guess I dozed off. I've got to say, I'm all for this whole napping thing. Seems like I never get a chance to just—you know —crash in the middle of the day."

"That's because the department works you too hard. I'm glad you're on leave. That way they can't bother you about this case. But speaking about the case—"

He sighed. "Now I'm putting everything together. I still had a sleepy brain. You're at the warehouse where they were making the floats."

"Yes but the floats and the flowers are long gone. I need to ask you the proper protocol for the item in my hand."

"Why am I suddenly wishing this were part of a dream? What protocol? What item?"

"I came to the warehouse to snoop around the desk that Sylvia worked at. It was all cleaned up so I thought well, that's that. Then I opened the desk drawer just in case and it contained broken pencils."

"Hope this gets more interesting," he chided.

"Ooh, someone's cranky after being woken from his nap. That sounds so cute, big, hunky Detective Jackson taking a nap. Anyhow, I pushed the drawer back in, but a piece of paper ripped and the drawer got caught. I pulled free the drawer and found an envelope, now slightly ripped, taped to the top of the drawer. Here's where it gets interesting, and where you say 'how the heck did the team miss that'? The envelope contains five one hundred dollar bills and a handwritten note. I've got it here so I'll read it to you. Last payment. I'm done with blackmail." I stopped talking and waited for a quick and shocked response. There was nothing. "Jax?"

"You're right," he said, drowsily, "how did the team miss that?"

"Here's my dilemma. Do I tape it carefully back to the same spot so your team can retrieve it, or do I just bring it home so they can come collect it and put it in evidence?"

"Since you've already taken it out, there's no sense putting it back. Bring it home. But take a few photos of the desk and the inside of the drawer. I'll use them to point out to my team just how easily they could have found it if they'd looked past their noses. Are you coming home soon?"

"Ah, you miss me. Wait, I'm not falling for that again. You're hungry."

"Both. I promise. Can you stop off and get me a cheese-burger and fries on the way home?"

"I think I can manage that. I'm on my way now. No more investigation. I've got a sleepy headed detective waiting for me to bring him food. By the way—"

"I haven't said one mean word to Edward all day. And get this, he's kind of angry about it. He keeps tossing out zingers. Since I wasn't taking the bait, he drifted upstairs to sulk."

"Can't win with ghosts. I'll see you soon."

CHAPTER 27

The aroma of burgers was making me hungry as I drove home. The blackmail envelope sat in the glove box clear of the greasy bags and drinks. It had been a far more productive outing than I'd anticipated. First, I was able to cross Sylvia's ex-husband off the suspect list. It seemed they'd had a turmoil filled breakup, one that could push someone to do something stupid and vindictive. But Ernie Franco had an alibi, and from the little I learned after talking to his coworker, it seemed intricate bomb building was not part of his skill set.

The jeep hit the rough part of the road that led to the Cider Ridge Inn. Instinctively, my arm shot out in the soccer mom protective reflex to make sure the cokes didn't fly through the front windshield. I turned up the gravel driveway that led to the inn. As it came into view, past the yellow birch and sugar maple trees that lined the front yard, a little sigh escaped me. It looked so proud and historic and welcoming with its newly painted portico and windows. The brick façade held onto its weathered beauty. It was the old house's way of letting everyone who visited know that it had seen far more history than any mere mortal. Just like a grandmother bragging that she'd earned each gray hair on her head, the manor seemed to be saying it had earned every bit of its patina.

Was I making a mistake keeping the historic gem to myself? "Ugh, stop debating it, Sunni. Just make a plan and stick to it." The phone rang as I reached for the food bags. It was Raine. Normally, I would have let it go to voicemail and called her back later, but I was feeling so indebted to my best friend, I picked it right up.

"Just checking in on Jackson. I'm waiting for my one o'clock tarot card reading. Evelyn's always late because she dreads coming here. She's always sure I'm going to give her some terrible news."

I laughed. "Then why does she do it?"

"I don't know," Raine said. "I guess it's like not going in for your physical because you're worried the doctor will have bad news. Then you go because you want to get ahead of the bad news. So how is the big guy?"

"Thanks to you, my dear friend, he's sitting in the kitchen, rested from a nap and waiting for me to bring his burgers inside."

"I don't deserve the credit. You're the one that made the call." She wasn't usually so humble when her predictions turned out right, but this particular prophecy was nothing else if not humbling. She had saved a man's life and in turn, saved mine. I just couldn't imagine a life without Jackson. I swallowed to rid myself of the newly formed lump. They were sort of constant in the last twenty-four hours.

"I wouldn't have made that call if you hadn't told me to do it, Raine. It's all on you. You saved Jackson's life. I'll never be able to repay you, which means I'm eternally in your debt."

A sniffle came through the phone. Raine wasn't a big crier, but her sniffle made my throat tighten again. Just like Jackson had advised, I'd been thinking hard on whether to reveal Edward to

Raine. I was sure she would appreciate it more than any gift I could give her. And what gift do you give someone who saved your loved one's life? Patchouli candles and a box of chocolates just didn't seem enough.

"My one o'clock just drove up," she sniffled briefly. "Now you've got me all choked up. Evelyn is going to freak out sure that my teary eyes mean she's going to face some dire situation in the near future. Oh, before I go—I have to ask, and I know you were in a frantic state of mind at that moment, but after you heard the explosion you asked the empty kitchen behind you if he was all right."

I sat back and a breath rushed out of me. I'd hoped she hadn't noticed. I was so scared, and since Edward seemed to have some sixth sense when it came to his descendant, I'd asked him if Jackson was all right.

At least Raine's unexpected question had softened the lump in my throat. I glanced up into the rearview to see my own eyes staring back at me. Tell her, Sunni. This is your chance. I dragged my eyes from the reflection and cleared my throat.

"I think I was talking to God. I probably don't do it enough, but at that moment, it seemed like a good time." My courage slipped away before I could tell her the truth. I just wasn't ready, and I wasn't sure it was a good idea. Like Jackson had said, the more people that knew, the more chances of it getting out to the world.

"I'll let you go," I said. "Talk to you later. And try not to freak out poor Evelyn."

Jackson had apparently been watching from the kitchen window and wondering why his burgers were still in the jeep and not in his stomach. The dogs had joined him on the front stoop, their tails wagging furiously. (The dogs, that is, although I could almost imagine a tail on Jackson when he spotted the greasy white bags in my hand.)

"I was worried," he said. "You pulled in, then you just sat in the jeep. Everything all right?"

"If you're asking about the burgers, they're fine. Just a little colder." I handed him the bags and walked to the door. "If you're asking about me, I just flat out lied to my best friend and the woman who saved your life." I kept talking as we walked to the kitchen.

The dogs trotted energetically behind us sure that this time the burgers in the bag were for them. I handed them each a treat. That seemed to let them down easily.

Jackson pulled two plates down from the cupboard. He looked much more himself this afternoon, rested and not shaken. "What did you lie about?"

Right then, the subject of the lie popped into view. He had pulled my copy of Wilkie Collins' *The Haunted Hotel* off the library shelf. I'd found a copy at a local charity event and thought it might relate to my life. However, there were few, if any, similarities. It seemed Edward was not your average ghost. At least not one that might be found in ghostly literature.

"This is a ridiculous book," Edward scoffed. "I see he's feeding himself yet again."

Jackson unwrapped a burger and held it up to admire. "Greasy, drippy and messy, just the way I like it. Would you like a taste, Gramps? Oh wait, that's right. Sorry."

I glowered at Jackson. Yesterday's shock was still coursing through my veins, but his comment was cruel. Poor Edward would never again enjoy the taste or aroma of a good meal. Just as he would never know the absolute luxury of diving into a soft bed after a long, hard day of work.

Jackson swallowed his first bite and lifted his napkin. It was definitely a one bite one wipe kind of burger. "You never said, what did you lie to Raine about?"

I looked pointedly at Edward. He was scowling at the book as he read it.

Jackson caught on… sort of. "You mean you kept up the lie about Cider Ridge not being haunted? That's hardly a lie since that's what you've been telling her the whole time."

"Haunted," Edward drawled. "A ridiculous word."

Jackson shrugged. "Lots of ridiculousness today."

"After the phone call with you ended—" merely talking about it sent a shudder through me. "I was beside myself. Edward seemed to have sensed you were in danger. Out of desperation, I asked if you were all right. Raine caught me talking to empty air." I shook my head. "Anyhow, I think I've made up my mind." I turned my focus to Edward since this involved him far more than Jackson. "I'm going to tell Raine. Not sure when but I owe her, and this would be so important to her. She's been working on talking to spirits her whole career. Now she can actually talk to one and find out what she had right and what she had wrong. It'll be like research for her."

Jackson shook his head but kept eating.

"It'll be fine, Jax. You'll see." I turned back to Edward. "What do you say?"

"I'm not sure what to say, but I don't want to spend hours talking to that silly woman, answering questions about my existence."

"Fine, I'll tell her she'll have limited interview time. And, of course, she'll have to keep it a secret. She won't be able to talk to her psychic and medium friends about you. That'll probably be hard, but I know I can trust Raine." I picked up my burger and released a sigh. "There. I feel a weight off my shoulders already." I took a bite and halfway through chewing I once again asked myself 'am I making the right decision'. Ugh, when did I become so darn indecisive?

CHAPTER 28

*I*t was a lovely spring night. A gentle breeze ruffled the trees and grasses in the pasture and a half full moon lent its glow to the landscape. The occasional male firefly popped up from the lush foliage trying to impress a female with its bright tail. From somewhere in the tall trees a hoot owl tooted to its mate.

I took Jackson's hand as we stepped out on the road. "This is the most perfect walk I've had in a long time. The weather is great, nature is wonderful, and I've got the best boyfriend in the world at my side." There it was again, that painful lump in my throat. This weekend could have been so dreadfully different. Instead, I had Jackson to myself for an entire two days. It was rare when he had the whole weekend off and even then, he would be on call. And the precinct never hesitated to call. So many plans disrupted but what happened this week could have disrupted them for good.

"I don't need to offer a penny for your thoughts," Jackson said quietly. He tugged my hand to pull me a little closer. My shoulder touched his now. "I already know what you're thinking."

"I'm not sure when I'm going to get over the abject horror of it all. Yet, you seem to be entirely past it, and you were the one who went through the actual explosion."

"Trust me, if a car backfires or someone sets off a firecracker, I'll probably duck for cover. But you forget, I face possible death every day I'm on the job. If I let this incident get to me, then I'd be turning in my badge."

I'd never voiced my thoughts on his job, but he gave me an opening. "Would that be so terrible? Turning in your badge? I'm being selfish I know, but I wouldn't shed too many tears if you resigned."

"What would I do?"

"Well, there's always hair commercials. And toothpaste commercials. Then that Hollywood smile wouldn't be wasted." I snapped my fingers. "That's it. Hollywood. Then I'd be dating a movie star. No, never mind. Hollywood is too far away, and it's filled with gorgeous women. You'd forget all about Sunni and her big old house."

"That would never happen," he assured me. However, I wasn't delusional. Movie stars rarely stayed with one spouse.

"What about farming? Since I'm not opening the inn, the property can and should be used for something else. I'm thinking lots of cuddly critters, some cool horses and a large vegetable patch. You could just strut around all day on your tractor in your boots and flannel shirts. And flannel shirts are a must. I'm just putting that out there right now."

A raccoon skittered out from a bush, stared at us through his cute little mask and turned right back around to hide.

"Have to admit, the whole thing sounds appealing."

"But?" I asked. "That statement was definitely a precursor to a but."

We both laughed like preadolescents at the sentence I'd concocted and the word but.

"*But*, I like my job, Sunni. It makes me who I am. I like catching bad guys. You, of all people, should know how satisfying it is to solve a murder."

"I do but the explosion, the frighteningly close call, it reminded me how easily I could lose you."

He stopped and pulled me into his arms. "I'm not going anywhere, Sunni." We kissed under the moonlight and amongst the lyrical sounds of nature. It always felt so right being in Jackson's arms. Unless his shirt vibrated, which it did. We parted and both stared at his shirt pocket.

"I thought you were on leave." I said.

"I am. This must be one of the other women in my life," he teased.

I smacked his arm and kept walking. He followed.

"Jackson here." He flipped it to speaker, so I knew it was about the case.

"Detective Jackson, thought you'd like to know we've just made an arrest," the voice on the other end said.

I scooted in closer not wanting to miss a word. I was disappointed that I wasn't going to be the one to solve the case, but I supposed, occasionally, I had to let the police have their moment in the sun. I badly wanted to ask who was arrested, but I couldn't let them know I was listening in.

"The suspect, an Arthur Andrews," the voice started

My hand flew to my mouth to muffle my gasp. It wasn't all that surprising, but it was always stunning to hear that it was someone on my list. With the amount of enemies Sylvia had it was a fairly easy list to form.

"He used to be on the city council," Jackson said. "What's the evidence you have?"

"Andrews confessed to planting the bomb on Ms. Franco's car."

Another gasp. This one earned an admonishing look from Jackson. I pulled the invisible zipper across my lips.

"Some of the witnesses mentioned that Sylvia had fired him from the Founders' Day Committee. Apparently, there was some bad blood between them all the way back from his time on the council. Ms. Franco worked at city hall."

I pointed to myself and mouthed the words 'I knew that' to Jackson. He rolled his eyes briefly.

"Turned out that Mr. Andrews was in the military. Explosives were his specialty. We showed up to talk to him, and he just put his hands out for the cuffs. What he didn't know was that his bomb nearly killed a detective." The officer on the other end chuckled. "Never seen someone turn so white so fast."

"Was his motive just that he didn't like the woman or that he lost his seat on the committee?" Jackson asked. He was taking all the words right out of my mouth. We were either so bonded we were channeling the same thoughts, or I'd gotten so good at detective work, I knew just what a professional would ask. I was hoping it was a little of both.

"Turns out, Ms. Franco was blackmailing Andrews for something that happened when they were both at city hall," the officer reported. "Ms. Franco's phone is in evidence. There are a number of texts between Andrews and the victim and most of them are cryptic, talking about meeting places and drop off locations."

Jackson looked up at me. This time I turned the invisible key to assure him I was staying quiet even though my feet were doing a little dance.

"It all came out in his confession. He had his hand in the till, so to speak, when he worked as treasurer. The victim had evidence that would prove his guilt, but instead of turning him in, she was blackmailing him for five hundred dollars a month. He said the whole thing left him so broke, he knew he had to get rid of her or turn himself in. It's just too bad he didn't choose the latter. Now, stealing from the treasury will be the lightest charge he's facing."

"As far as the blackmailing evidence goes," Jackson said, "I've got something to add to that, something the team missed. Have one of the officers drive out to Cider Ridge Inn in the morning to pick it up."

"Wow, I thought they'd done a thorough job. I'll have to talk to the team."

"Speaking of evidence—it's obvious he attempted murder on Ms. Franco, but do you have enough to connect him to the actual murder, the carbon monoxide poisoning?" Jackson asked. "We don't want him to get a reduced sentence for attempted murder when he actually killed her. He really wanted her dead."

"We're working on that now and hoping we can get a confession on that too. How are you feeling, Detective Jackson?"

"Great and now it seems you don't need me for this case. I'll be glad to face that guy down in the courtroom."

"I think we all will. I'll let you get back to resting. We'll keep you posted."

"Please do." Jackson hung up. "Did you know the part about him being in the military and a bomb expert?"

"I did not know that. I hadn't really been concentrating on Arthur Andrews. The man nearly plowed into me when I was walking into the warehouse with one of the volunteers the day before the parade. He was grumbling and angry, ready to commit murder, one might say. Marilyn, the volunteer, filled me in on the tension between Arthur and Sylvia. She said Arthur got thrown off the committee because he was dating Christy Jacobs, Sylvia's rival. Now, I'm thinking she wanted him off because he was a thief."

"Doesn't sound as if Sylvia Franco was exactly a good citizen either," Jackson noted. "Blackmailing takes a pretty devious mind."

"Look where it got her." We headed back toward the inn. "I'm sort of sad the case is over. I must say, I was at the parade all morning while the floats got ready, and I never saw Arthur Andrews once."

"Since he was up to something sinister, maybe he was trying to stay unseen or maybe he had on a disguise."

"Yeah, maybe," I said. But I wasn't convinced. Was it possible two people wanted Sylvia Franco dead and only one succeeded?

CHAPTER 29

Sunday morning usually meant coffee with my sisters. This morning Nick arrived with them, and Emily brought a batch of freshly baked cinnamon rolls. As much as I would have preferred a different topic, everyone was interested in hearing about the near miss explosion.

Nick had finished his roll first. "What were the shock waves like? Were they strong enough to launch you into the air?"

Jackson didn't seem to mind talking about it. He'd basically put it all behind him. I'd only heard it through the phone, and I still relived those horrifying seconds every time I picked up my phone.

Jackson sat back with his coffee. I realized then how nice it was having all of us around the table for Sunday cinnamon rolls and coffee. Jackson was almost always at work on Sunday morning, and Nick rarely joined us for our sister coffee chat, both because he was not a sister and because there were always so many chores on the farm.

"To be honest, Nick, it all happened so fast, I can't remember fully if I jumped first or if the waves hit me. All I remember is a lot of debris pelting me and my ears ringing as if I'd sat up front at a twenty-four hour rock concert."

"Did your life pass before your eyes?" Nick asked.

"Nick, seriously?" Emily asked.

"He had a near death experience. It always happens in movies, so I wondered if the whole thing was real."

Jackson rubbed his unshaven chin between his thumb and forefinger. "Hmm, let me think. You know, I remember thinking Sunni is going to be so mad if I die." He looked across the table at me. "And I saw her face. I could still hear her voice too."

"That's because I was screaming into the phone. Did you really see my face?" I felt my cheeks warm with a blush. We never flirted or got mushy in front of a whole table of people.

Then, for a second, everyone faded away, even the ghost who had been sulking about the Sunday morning intrusion since everyone walked in, disappeared, and it was just Jackson and me at the big farm table.

"Yes, Bluebird. I think yours was the only face, so if that was my whole life passing before my eyes, I approve of it readily."

"Aww," Lana said abruptly, "and all this cuteness is my cue to leave. I've got work to do. Since I am once again a fifth wheel, I think I'm going to go online and buy myself a cardboard cutout of a man, someone I can drag along with me to these little get-togethers."

"Lana, don't go," I said to her as she leaned over and grabbed another cinnamon roll.

"No, no, I don't want your pity. That would be worse than the whole fifth wheel thing. Besides, I have fifteen centerpieces to make, so I'm going home to my most loyal partner, the hot glue gun. I'll see all of you later." She walked over and kissed Jackson's cheek. "Glad you're sitting here all in one piece, Detective Jackson."

Jackson grabbed her hand before she made a clean getaway.

He gave her one of those semi-smiles that was almost as spectacular as the full one. "He's an idiot."

Lana nodded. "I couldn't agree more."

I winked at Jackson to let him know I approved of everything
about him. He might not have understood all that in the brief
gesture. But it was true.

"Well, Em, I think we should get back to the farm. The goats
and chickens won't clean their own pens."

"No?" Emily asked. "And why not? Maybe we should teach
them."

"Jackson, do you want another cinnamon roll?" Emily
lowered the tray in front of him.

"Don't mind if I do," Jackson said cheerily.

Edward clucked his tongue. "Does the man ever stop eating?"

Jackson secretly held the cinnamon roll up in a silent toast to
Edward. However, his phone rang before he could take a bite.

I walked Emily and Nick to the door. Emily stayed behind for
a second. "How are you doing? You looked a little piqued when
the men were talking about the explosion."

"I'm fine but I'm not a hundred percent over it yet. Thank
goodness for Raine."

"Yes, we need to bake her a cake or have a little party for
her." Emily's blue eyes always sparkled at the mention of a
possible party.

"I like that idea," I said. "We'll talk to Lana and see what will
work best. By the way—"

Emily bit her lip for a second. "Maybe she's taking this harder
than we realized."

"That's what I was thinking."

"I'll check in on her later," Emily said. "You have your patient
to look after." She hugged me and hurried out to catch up to
Nick.

I rinsed coffee cups while Jackson finished his phone call. It definitely had something to do with the Sylvia Franco case because her name was being tossed around and Arthur Andrews came up too.

I tried to bend my ear in the direction of the call but sabotaged my own efforts by washing cups in the sink. The water and clink of china muted the conversation.

He finally hung up. I turned off the water, dried my hands and spun around. "What's new?"

"Andrews planted the bomb to kill Sylvia, but he had nothing to do with her death."

I clapped once, a little too excitedly. It meant the case wasn't closed, which was bad for the police but good for this part-time investigator.

Jackson smiled and shook his head. "You're supposed to say, that's too bad, dear."

I laughed. "When have I ever called you dear? I think I'll start. Or maybe I'll go with dearest. Dearest, what would you like for lunch today? Dearest—"

He held up his hand. "Jax works fine."

"Let's go outside, and you can tell me all about it. The dogs are getting antsy to terrify some squirrels, and the fresh air will do you good... dearest. You're right. Doesn't work."

"Nothing wrong with dearest," Edward commented. "I used to call all my women acquaintances dearest."

I stopped in front of the hearth where he was still thumbing through the ghost novel but with obvious distaste. "Do you hear the irony in that statement? Dearest implies that person is more dear than anyone else, but if you were calling *all*—and we'll debate that at another time, Mr. must try all the fish in the sea—of them dearest, then the term meant nothing. It was just two syllables strung together to refer to a person whose name you probably forgot. I refer you back to the word *all*."

Edward had a teasing glint in his eyes. "It's so easy. I'm pleased to see you're back to your old, contentious self."

Jackson chuckled on the way out. "He got you good."

"Oh shut up." Another glorious spring day awaited us outside. The dogs pushed past barking and running toward an anticipated squirrel though none were visible. At least not to the human eye.

Jackson and I strolled around the yard.

"How do they know Andrews wasn't responsible for Sylvia's death?"

"I admit, when they told me, I thought why would he go through constructing a highly complex bomb if he was just going to kill her with carbon monoxide." He paused to throw the stick Newman had brought him. "He had the detonator wired to go off at the exact frequency of her car remote. That took some knowhow and elaborate planning. But why go through all the trouble if you were just going to seal her up in a carbon monoxide filled box anyhow. And why wouldn't he have removed the bomb since carbon monoxide did the trick?"

"Right, I hadn't thought of all that," I said. "I just kept thinking that I'd never seen Arthur Andrews at the parade ware-house that day. But that makes a lot of sense. Leaving the bomb made him much easier to catch, and he risked causing other deaths, even to police officers. If his first attempt succeeded, he could have disarmed the bomb, and the police would have had a harder case."

"Exactly. That was what he told the interrogators. He also had an alibi. Andrews works at an accounting firm in the city. He knew that Sylvia would be at the parade route at the crack of dawn to make sure the parade started on time. He followed her to find out where she parked. Then he waited for her to walk the few blocks to the warehouse. He got out and rigged her car with the bomb, then headed off to work. According to the accounting office, he was there from seven until four the day of the parade."

"And they didn't pull out the floats until seven, so he couldn't have sabotaged the dragon."

"Right. Of course, he's still in a great deal of trouble."

I looked up at him. "But Sylvia's real killer is still out there. I just hope I can catch the culprit before my story deadline."

He cleared his throat. "Uh, *you* can catch them?"

"Who else is going to do it? After all, the county's number one detective is recuperating at the Cider Ridge Inn." I decided to pull him off the subject, so I wouldn't get the usual lecture about staying out of trouble. Our stroll had taken us to the back of the house. There were acres of tall grasses growing in fresh and green for spring. I covered a sneeze. There were also plenty of pollen heavy weeds, but the insects and birds seemed to be enjoying them. "I'm thinking a red traditional barn right there and a cute chicken coop closer to the house so I can collect eggs before breakfast."

"Doesn't your sister already provide you with so many eggs you don't know what to do with them all?"

"Yes but I've heard they taste much better if you collect them yourself." I took hold of his hand. "What do you think? You could have a horse."

"I must admit, that would be cool. And I do like wearing flannel."

CHAPTER 30

$\mathcal{J}$ ackson had a soccer game to watch, so I was just as glad to get out of the house. It hadn't taken long to find Brandy's phone number on the county website. She was listed as personal assistant to planning manager Sylvia Franco. Brandy answered hesitantly but was friendly enough after I told her it was Sunni from the *Junction Times*. I told her I was planning to add a piece in the article that highlighted all of Sylvia's achievements. I knew Brandy was open and chatty, and I hoped to pry some more information out of her.

I wasn't surprised to see that Brandy lived in a cute little cottage with daisies and yellow roses planted around the front yard. I hadn't noticed a ring on her finger and her car was the only one in the driveway, so I assumed she lived alone. A small dog barked wildly as I walked up to the front door.

Brandy opened the door with a sunny smile. She seemed to be one of those people who was always happy. That couldn't have been easy working for Sylvia Franco, but her positive attitude might just have been the reason they made a good team.

"Hello," she chirped, then she turned to the small white

poodle mix who was still barking. "Fudgy-poo, that's enough. She's come for a visit so be nice." Brandy turned back to me. "He barks but he doesn't bite. Not unless you're wearing a uniform," she added as I stepped inside.

"Then I'm glad I left my uniform in the closet this morning."

Brandy giggled. She was definitely more of a giggler than a laugher. I was somewhat surprised to see that she was in such a cheery mood this morning. "Would you like some coffee or tea? I have a delicious citrusy orange tea."

"That would be wonderful." Her cozy little house was decorated with a lot of floral prints. Charming paintings of country landscapes hung on the walls in the front room. Vertical pink striped wallpaper covered the walls of her small kitchen and roses were stenciled on the wooden cabinets. It was exactly how I expected it to look, froo froo but with style. It wasn't for me but I liked it.

I sat at her round kitchen table. Fudgy-poo trotted into the kitchen and flopped down in a bed near his food bowl. "Love the pink and white wallpaper," I said.

"Thanks. It was a little bold of me, but I just love the way it looks. Like a gentlewoman's parlor," she said in a posh English accent that—to my ear—one that heard a posh accent all day long—sounded pretty spot on.

She set the table with two tea cups. A rich orange scent wafted off the tea bags. She returned to the stove for the kettle. "I heard that Arthur Andrews has been arrested for the murder." She poured the hot water, returned the kettle to the stove and sat across from me still wearing the smile she wore when she opened the door. "It doesn't surprise me. Arthur hated Sylvia. I wouldn't be surprised if Christy had her hand in it too. She hated Sylvia as much as Arthur, and since they were dating, it makes sense that they might have been conspiring together."

I sat forward with interest. I hadn't expected her to toss

Christy's name out there, but it made some sense. Christy was at the warehouse all morning and could have carried out the terrible deed at Arthur's request. Maybe the bomb really was just a backup plan, an elaborate one at that.

"Brandy, did Sylvia know she had a heart defect?"

Brandy twirled her tea bag around. Citrus scent filled the air. "I think she might have mentioned that to me once. But she kept fit." Brandy sighed. "She was always trying to get me to take better care of myself. I'm going to start a new diet Monday. I'm determined to get fit... for Sylvia." Her face dropped and a rare frown formed on her lips. Her shoulders jerked and a sniffle followed. "People hated her, but they didn't know that she had a good side, a generous side." She lifted her face and blotted her eyes dry with a napkin. "Sylvia helped me with some money when my mom was sick with cancer. The bills piled up. We were going to lose the house." Her eyes swept around. "I inherited it from my mom after she died. If Sylvia hadn't stepped in to help, the bank would have swooped in to take it."

I thought about the extra money Sylvia was making on the side through blackmail. She was breaking Arthur's bank account, but it made me feel better to think that she was at least doing something good with the money.

"That was kind of her. I'm sure you feel her loss keenly."

"Every hour of the day." Brandy took a loud sip of tea.

"But then it seems you earned it. Forgive me for saying so, but I witnessed her being rather harsh, cruel even on several occasions."

Brandy set the cup down. "I was used to it. I guess because I knew she had a good side, it was easier to ignore the bossy side. She went through dozens of assistants before she hired me. Don't get me wrong, it was a stressful job, but she paid well and she was a friend when I needed it."

My ears perked up. "She had to fire a lot of other assistants?" Was there an entire list of ex-assistants with horror stories and possible vendettas?

She waved her hand. "I exaggerate. My mom used to scold me for it all the time. Not a lot of assistants but several. At least that's what I've heard."

"But Sylvia did have a lot of enemies. Or is that an exaggeration too?"

"That one is mostly true. There's her ex-husband and Christy and Andrew, of course. Let's just say, Sylvia managed to anger a lot of people on her climb up the ladder. She was moving up fast in the city planner's office. You don't get that far without stepping on some toes. Even Benny, who is kind to everyone, tended to grumble whenever she ordered him to do something. I almost expected him to quit, but he's a trooper."

The mention of Benny had brought up something important, something that I'd been ignoring. "The morning of the parade, just before it was time for the drivers to move the floats to the line, Sylvia texted Benny telling him to get some floral wire. Somehow, he got locked in the supply closet. That was why Sylvia had to drive for him."

"Yes, I remember searching all over for him." Her chin dropped. "You don't think the person was actually trying to kill Benny, do you?" I was slightly annoyed with myself for not even having that cross my mind, but it wouldn't make sense. It seemed the killer purposely locked Benny in so that Sylvia would have to drive the float.

"I think it's more likely that the killer locked Benny inside the closet. Did you know that Sylvia sent him back for some wire? Do you know what she needed it for?"

Fudgy-poo sensed that Brandy was finished with her tea. He waddled over and jumped right into her lap. She gave him a little squeeze. "They're always so needy. Do you have dogs, Miss Taylor?"

"Please, call me Sunni, and yes, I have two very needy dogs as well. They're a little too big to be lap dogs. Not that they don't occasionally attempt it."

"You were asking about the wire. I honestly have no idea what she needed it for. I can only assume some last minute repair. It was strange that she sent him back, but there was so much commotion that morning, she was texting everyone."

I remembered Sylvia standing at her manager's station working the phone as well as issuing orders throughout the building.

Brandy's forehead bunched up into little straight lines. "If the police already have the killer, why are you still asking about her enemies?" Apparently, it only just dawned on her that, so far, my interview had nothing to do with Sylvia's accomplishments. It wasn't my place to change the narrative.

"You're right. It's just that I was at the warehouse that morning, and I never saw Arthur Andrews. Maybe you saw him? You know him better than me." Arthur already had an alibi for that morning, but I was curious what she thought. "How could he have done it if he wasn't even there?"

"It was so hectic, and there were so many people pouring in and out of the warehouse, I could easily have missed him. But that was why I mentioned the possibility that Christy was an accomplice. She had access to everything and was there all morning."

Brandy was definitely game for throwing Christy under the bus. The police had interviewed Christy, but it seemed they hadn't considered her a suspect. What if Brandy was right? Maybe Christy was in charge of plan A, and Arthur was covering plan B.

"Now," Brandy said with her sweet smile returning, "you

wanted to hear about some of Sylvia's accomplishments? They're quite extensive, so you'll want to write them down."

I pulled out my notepad. "Yes, that would be wonderful." Sometimes my little white lies came back to bite me in the bottom.

CHAPTER 31

*J*ackson had gone back to his place Sunday night. He was hoping to cut short his leave now that there was still a killer to catch, but the chief had given him a hard no. I was relieved. He was still badly bruised on his side, and his movements were slower than usual. For his line of work, you needed to feel a hundred percent. He grumbled in frustration as I drove him home. Napping and taking leisurely lunches was nice for a few days, but they could get boring fast, especially for someone like Jackson who was always in the action.

I walked into the newsroom. Myrna looked up with one of her 'where have you been' looks, which meant Prudence was in one of her moods. Which mood was still anyone's guess because she had so many of them. Parker was busy picking the crumbs of his muffin off his tie and pushing them into his mouth.

"Morning," I said, pointedly.

"Morning," Myrna answered. She tilted her head toward the closed office door.

"Is it bad?" I whispered.

"Is it ever good?" Parker asked plainly and loudly, even after I had taken care to whisper.

Prudence's door flew open. "Sunni, you're finally here." I glanced with some annoyance at the newsroom clock that assured me I was right on time. "I'm sure you've heard all about the terrible tragedy at the parade."

"I was there for the whole thing."

"Good, come into my office. We need to talk."

I glanced at Myrna to see if she got the sense it was a good talk or a bad one. Myrna just shrugged and smiled weakly.

Prudence sat at her desk. "Close the door and pull up a chair."

I shut the door and walked up to the chairs in front of her desk. They were upholstered and much more comfortable than the ones Parker used to keep for guests. I was trying to predict what she might say by reading her expression, but it wasn't working.

Prudence adjusted the pearls on her neck. The necklace was just a few pearls short of being the right length for her pillowy neck. It was biting into her skin, but she didn't seem to mind. "First of all, it was just shocking to hear the news. I knew Sylvia Franco. We used to play in the same bridge club. She tried hard to be one of those society women, you know, hanging out at the country club for brunch and joining all the important clubs." Prudence and I had different ideas of which clubs in town were important. "She had quite a few connections at city hall, so, natu- rally, most of the women in my social circle were happy to invite her in. Her manners were a bit brusque, and she definitely rubbed people the wrong way. As is evident in that someone murdered her." She tried to adjust the necklace again. It was starting to make me uncomfortable, like I was choking. I casually reached up and tugged at the collar of my blouse. "I didn't mind her but then I hardly had any interactions with the woman."

"I agree," I said. "Her manner was abrasive, and she had quite a few enemies."

Prudence laughed that society woman's deep, throaty laugh. "You young people always like those extreme terms. She had some people who weren't her friends, but I don't know if they could be labeled enemies."

It wasn't worth the time to debate her on it. I just smiled and nodded, and again, discreetly tugged at my collar as I watched the pearls disappear under her neck folds.

"I understand Arthur Andrews has been arrested for killing Sylvia Franco." Prudence did the little thing that she did with her lips, rolled them in primly, when she thought she was ahead of me on a scoop.

It looked as if I was going to have to unfurl those prim lips. "Actually, he was arrested for the bomb incident and attempted murder, but he didn't kill Sylvia."

Prudence looked stunned, confused. "I understand there was a car explosion near the parade." She was more out of the loop than I expected. "I heard an officer was nearly killed."

I blinked at her for a few seconds trying to decide if I should mention exactly which officer had nearly died, but I found just bringing it up caused me to get weepy eyed. At the moment, I had the upper hand on my boss, and I wasn't about to waste it.

"The car that exploded belonged to Sylvia. Arthur Andrews confessed to setting the bomb. He was trying to kill Sylvia, only someone else got to her first during the parade."

Prudence sat back hard enough the cushions on her chair released a soft sigh. "Oh my, I had no idea. I knew Arthur Andrews when he was on city council. There were rumors of scandal that forced him out. I never heard exactly what those were. Did they involve Sylvia Franco?"

"I'm not entirely sure which scandal you're speaking of, but I have found some information that links Sylvia to Arthur in a blackmail plot."

Prudence's eyes lit up. "How intriguing. Blackmail should make for an interesting article." Prudence straightened the papers on her desk even though they were already sitting in neat piles with edges parallel to the desk edge. "I've been learning through trial and error on this whole newspaper business. I have discovered that, as distasteful as it is, scandal and murder do attract readers."

I nodded. "Human nature, I'm afraid. Like the accident on the highway, it's hard to look away." I was trying to tamp down my excitement. It seemed she was heading in a good direction with this but then I'd been tricked and disappointed before. Knowing Prudence as I now did, she might very well turn the opposite direction and insist nothing negative ever be printed again in her precious newspaper. I hoped that wasn't the case, but I had to wait for her to once again give a little tug to her pearls. I kept expecting them to break off in her hand.

"I don't remember this necklace being so tight but then I haven't worn these pearls in years. I just thought they went with the outfit."

"They look nice with that pastel pink dress," I noted.

"Yes, I thought so too." She moved her head, and the pearls disappeared once again. "All right, let's get to it," she said. "I think it would do wonders for our circulation numbers if we, well, you, could find out who killed Sylvia. If we got the scoop on the murder of such a prominent citizen, I think we could raise the price of our ads." For Prudence, a woman with seemingly unlimited financial resources, it all still came down to one thing— money. "Now, I know it's a difficult assignment, and I certainly don't want you to put yourself in any kind of danger but you've proven yourself to be very good at this sort of stuff." She said the last part almost as if it left a bad taste in her mouth, as if chasing murderers was somehow lowly and not for general society. "If you get this story, the lead reporter job is yours." She sat back with satisfaction and a grin as if she'd just offered me the world on a platter rather than the *possibility* of having my old job back, one that I'd earned a hundred times over. And all I had to do to get it was catch a killer. But I loved a good challenge, and since finding Sylvia's killer was already on my to do list I nodded.

"I'll hold you to that," I said.

"Perfect." She crossed her fingers and placed them on her desk. The grin and the crossed fingers reminded me of some campy villain thrilled that the world conquering was going their way. "Now get out there and get the scoop."

I hopped up.

"But stay safe. There are a lot of crazy people out there apparently," she added before I left the room.

CHAPTER 32

It took only a bit of research to discover that Christy Jacobs worked at city hall. I could only assume that was where the two women met and initially started their fierce rivalry. Christy worked in the records office. Depending on how close she and Arthur were, there was a good chance she was not working, but I couldn't pass up the opportunity to talk to her. What if she was home fretting about being implicated in Sylvia's murder? Maybe she was at home crying her eyes out about her boyfriend's arrest. Maybe she had already packed and hopped a flight to Mexico or some exotic place where she could hide from the authorities. Or maybe she was standing right behind the records counter. Fortunately, the last scenario was the right one.

I got in line behind two other people waiting for records. Meeting her at work was not ideal, but it would have to do. My lead reporter job was on the line. Prudence was clever. She knew exactly the right carrot to dangle to push me full speed ahead on the case.

Fortunately, I was still the only person in line by the time I reached the window.

"What can I do for you?" Christy looked up from her computer and lowered her reading glasses. "It's you. You're the reporter." She shook her head. "I have nothing to say to the newspaper. Arthur and I were only dating for the last few months. I'm just glad I learned what a monster he was before things got serious. I didn't care for him that much anyhow. He was a terrible dresser and he cussed a lot." Her voice trembled. She pressed her fingers to her lips to calm herself. It seemed I'd gotten lucky and caught her at a vulnerable time when she needed to air her feelings. I'd stepped into the role of makeshift therapist many times in interviews. I was particularly happy to do so right now.

"This must have all been terribly shocking to you. First, the calamitous parade, Sylvia's murder and now Arthur's arrest."

She reached across to a box of tissues and pulled one free. "It's been a very trying few days. Worst of all—" she paused to wipe her nose. "Worst of all, the police brought me in for questioning. They seemed to think I was some sort of accomplice. I told them I had nothing to do with Sylvia's death. We weren't friends, but I'm not a murderer. I'm a mother for goodness sake." She wiped her nose again. "Anyhow, I had an alibi. I was working with two volunteers still trying to repair the damage to the tail." She blinked at me through teary eyes. "You were there. You saw that the float had been sabotaged. It was Sylvia. After her death, some of her volunteers came over to confess. She'd made them do it. She told them they'd never work on the Founders' Day floats again if they refused. The volunteers who work on those floats look forward to the event every year. No one wants to lose their spot on the volunteer list. Sylvia could be very vicious when she put her mind to it."

I thought about what Brandy had told me. "I heard that she had a good, generous side as well."

A dry laugh shot from her mouth. "Sylvia Franco? She didn't have a generous bone in her body."

"This is probably not mine to tell, but Brandy mentioned Sylvia helped her financially when her mother was sick. She helped Brandy save her house." I wasn't sure why I told her. I suppose I thought it would be nice to get one decent story out about the woman. After all, a hard-working, energetic woman was dead, and her children were without a mother. I hated to think her legacy as a shrew was all people would remember.

Christy looked skeptical about the story. "Brandy, that poor woman, she was always the center of Sylvia's abuse. I don't know how she put up with it. I'm happy to hear that Sylvia helped her out, but it might have been more to ease her own conscience than to help Brandy."

It seemed Christy was not going to accept any possibility that deep down Sylvia was a decent person. "Christy, did you see Benny the morning of the parade?"

"Benny? Of course, he was everywhere. Sylvia had him running around like his hair was on fire."

I wasn't sure if Christy knew about the supply closet or not. If she did, I didn't want to alert her to the fact that I was ferreting out information that might help solve the case. "I was with the dragon float when Sylvia called for all drivers to get in their cars. No one could find Benny. When was the last time you saw him?"

She moved her chin side to side in thought. "That's right. How could I forget? Sylvia had once again sent him on an errand. He walked out ahead of me. He was going to the dragon float. Then he got a text from Sylvia. He spun around so fast, he nearly crashed into me. He was shaking his head mumbling something about Sylvia running him ragged and needing floral wire. He went back into the warehouse. That was the last I saw him. Twenty minutes later, everyone was asking if we'd seen

Benny. I let them know he went back into the warehouse, but no one could find him."

"You left the warehouse behind Benny," I said, "Do you remember who was still in the building as you were leaving?"

She shrugged. "Everyone was outside helping move the floats to the starting line. The place was empty." A woman walked into the records office. It seemed my interview time was up. "Wait," she said before I could thank her and leave. "Brandy was still at the manager's station. I remember because I asked her if she was going to ride on the float and she said no. She looked really sad about it too. It figured Sylvia would deny her that."

"What was Brandy doing?"

"Just straightening up I think." Christy seemed to be catching on to my line of questioning. She narrowed her eyes. "You can't possibly think Brandy caused Sylvia's death?"

"No, I'm just trying to get every angle of that morning. Thanks so much for you time. I'll let you get back to work."

I bustled out of the records office. A theory was coming together in my head with all the strands still as frail as tissue, but they were clinging to each other at one central character— Sylvia's doting assistant, Brandy.

CHAPTER 33

I pulled up to Brandy's house and was glad to see her car in the driveway. On the way, I'd stopped and bought some donuts. I thought going with the friendly *figured you could use a treat and a chat* path might get her to open up. When Christy mentioned that Brandy had been the last person in the warehouse as she left to help move the floats, something else occurred to me. Sylvia had left her phone at the manager's station. Something told me an assistant might very well know the passcode, if there even was a passcode. Lana never bothered with one because she said it was a nuisance.

I headed up to the front door with my disarming box of assorted donuts. Fudgy-poo was barking before I even reached the door. I knocked and the door swung open a minute later. I then saw the reason for Fudgy-poo's exuberance. Brandy was wearing a straw hat and sunglasses. She had a leash in her hand. "Miss Taylor, I wasn't expecting you." She smiled at the donut box.

I lifted it. "Just a little thank you for sitting with me yesterday."

Fudgy-poo had shifted to a growl when he saw me, but as the aroma of donuts wafted into the house he sat at attention and wriggled his nose. Even the leash was not as important as the fragrant box in the stranger's hands.

"I was happy to do it. I'm glad people will be able to read about Sylvia's accomplishments. It will be like a nice eulogy. So many people have negative opinions of her."

Brandy's attitude was making it harder to see her as a suspect. The second half of our Sunday morning chat had been about all the good things Sylvia had done at city hall and in the planning office. She also worked at charity events and ran a food can donation drive at the school for families in need. Brandy had narrated it all with a sparkle in her eyes. She was proud to have been Sylvia's assistant through most of it. If Christy hadn't mentioned that Brandy was the last person in the building, I never would have considered Sylvia's loyal assistant as the killer. On top of that, in general, Brandy was just too sweet to plot a murder. But I'd learned more than once with murder you should never use a 'book's cover', as they say, to check the title off the list.

"I'm glad to write that eulogy," I said. "I also thought you could use a friend at this time. After all, you spent all your work days at Sylvia's side. I'm sure you miss her a lot."

Brandy nodded slowly. "It's been hard. I don't have a job now either. The city planner promised he'd find a spot for me in the office."

"Great. I'm glad that'll work out for you." We were still stuck awkwardly in the door. "I see you were about to take the dog out. I can just leave these here."

"Nonsense. I can't eat all the donuts alone. It just so happens that I'm brewing a fresh pot of coffee. Why don't you go on into the kitchen and pour yourself a cup. Fudgy-poo generally does his business by the time we get to the end of the block. We should be back shortly. I'd ask you along but"—she dropped her voice to a whisper—"he is really self-conscious about going number two. Even I have to pretend to look the other way."

"If you're sure?" I was already stepping inside. My mind went straight to the possibility of having her place to myself for a few minutes. It was terrible that I jumped right into the notion that I could snoop around, but how else was I going to find out whether gentle, cheery little Brandy was a cold-blooded killer?

"Absolutely. The sugar and cream are next to the coffee pot." She put on her sunglasses and hooked up the dog's leash. "We'll only be a few minutes, then we can chat over donuts and coffee." She practically skipped out the door. The whole scene made me suddenly sick with guilt.

Brandy was excited to have a friendly chat. I might have been entirely wrong, but something told me she didn't have a lot of friends. It sounded as if it had been just Brandy and her mom, which even cut out the possibility that she had siblings. Here I was posing as a friend, and all I wanted to know was whether or not Brandy killed her boss. Maybe this was one of those cases that was better left unsolved? After all, they had one person in custody who had tried to kill Sylvia with a bomb. Maybe that was enough.

I trudged to the kitchen with my donuts. A few seconds earlier they smelled of maple and sugar and deep-fried goodness, but now they smelled of betrayal. If the police hadn't considered Brandy a suspect, should I? The woman had to put up with a lot of abuse. Yet she still found good things to say about her harsh boss. It was truly the first time I felt awful about possibly solving a case. Then it occurred to me, I was still far from solving it. I could do a bit of snooping. With any luck, I'd find nothing. A quick snoop might help take Brandy off the list for good, then my guilty conscience could just slink away feeling stupid.

I set down the box of donuts and returned to the front room. The flowery décor reminded me that Brandy was not the killer type. She had a glossy white desk tucked in a corner of the room. Her laptop was sitting open on top. Framed photos hung above the desk. They were of Brandy and an older woman. The woman looked so much like her, I could easily deduce it was her mom. Each photo was taken at a vacation destination, on a white sand beach, beneath some large sequoias and in front of an amusement park. They looked incredibly close as if they were each other's best friend. Brandy must have been devastated when she died.

I glanced out the window. There was no sign of Brandy and her little dog. I always felt bad when I snooped through personal belongings but never as much when I was just perusing the search history on someone's computer. Somehow, technology always blurred that border between something personal and something that was far more public. At least that was what I told myself as I crept over to the little desk with the laptop. I smiled thinking she was just like me, using sticky notes to remember small things like take the bread out of the freezer and dentist appointment next Tuesday. I tended to stick mine to the bathroom mirror, but Brandy had them stuck on the edge of her desk. All of them were notes about things I would expect, turn off the backyard sprinkler, order dog treats on Amazon, nothing specific about murdering the boss at the parade.

I wiggled the mouse and immediately discovered that her homepage had timed out. I needed to enter a password to get in. I was almost relieved that I had an excuse not to snoop, but the journalist side of me couldn't give up so easily. I looked around the room for a clue into what her password might be. I had no idea what her birthday was, and I didn't know her mom's name. Then it hit me. If Brandy was like me with sticky notes maybe we had other things in common—like using pet names for passwords. And, as far as I knew, she only had the one pet.

I leaned over and typed Fudgy into the password space. It

was wrong. I typed in the full name Fudgy-poo. (I could only imagine the looks on my dogs' faces if I tried to call them Fudgy-poo or poo attached to any word, for that matter.) It worked. I was in. Now I liked her even more and wanted more for my hunch to be wrong.

I pulled down the bar that showed her search history. My entire wish that I wouldn't find anything that implicated her fell apart.

Directly below a search for dog supplements and dog groomers were the words 'how does carbon monoxide kill people'? What if she searched this after Sylvia died to see how it happened? It made sense. Maybe this meant nothing, or maybe it was wishful thinking.

A bark in the near distance caused me to lurch forward, click out of the browsing history and race back to the kitchen. I quickly poured myself a cup and plucked a chocolate glazed out of the box. I took a bite and was taking a second when the front door opened.

Brandy was just finishing telling Fudgy-poo that he did a great job on the walk. She was congratulating him, which made me like her more. Darn her charming innocence. Again, I was jumping to conclusions based on a search history. Everyone had odd outliers in their search history. Just the other day I was looking up cyanide poisoning from apricot pits because I'd eaten three apricots and discovered that Newman had dug the pits out of the trash to chew up like dog treats. (One would think I never fed them, and they had to rely on garbage digging for sustenance.) I realized after I typed the question, a frantic dog mom making sure I wasn't going to have to get his stomach pumped, I laughed thinking what if the police found my computer and saw I was researching cyanide poisoning. It made sense that Brandy would be searching the subject. Death by carbon monoxide was rare. Naturally, people would be curious to see how it could happen. There were probably a number of computers in Firefly Junction with the same subject in their search history after the parade disaster.

I was deep in thought and hadn't noticed that Fudgy had returned to the kitchen but Brandy had not. I assumed she was taking off her sunglasses and hat. I leaned down to pet Fudgy-poo. Brandy's flat gray shoes came into view.

I sat up. "I hear he was a good boy."

Brandy smiled faintly, but her expression was harder than usual. "Were you looking at my computer?" she asked. "One of my sticky notes was on the floor."

CHAPTER 34

The quick bite of donut had given me just enough time to come up with a plausible response to Brandy's thinly veiled accusation that I'd been tampering with her computer. Her usually round cheeked, sweet grin had pulled into a straight-lipped, angry frown.

"I'm sorry," I said with an exaggerated donut swallow, "I must have knocked it off when I was admiring the photos of you and your mom. At least I think it's your mom because you both have the exact same lovely smiles." A little sugarcoating never hurt when one had been caught red-handed. "Where was that amusement park? That roller coaster in the background looked scary. I'm never good on those rides. I always end up feeling sick to my stomach." I was blathering on just like any totally guilty person might do.

"It was in Tennessee," she said through a tight jaw. Her entire demeanor had changed. I'd seen her being scolded without merit by Sylvia, but she'd never looked tense and angry like she did now in her cute flowery kitchen with the pink and white stripes.

She turned to her coffee pot. Her round shoulders looked sharper than usual.

I pinched off another piece of donut. It was the last thing I wanted at that tense moment, but I wanted to keep up the casual, chatty girls with donuts ambience.

She put the coffee pot down hard enough that the coffee sloshed around. Much harder and the glass pot would have broken into pieces. Fudgy-poo seemed to sense something was wrong. (As a doggie mom, I was sure it had more to do with the fact that he didn't receive a treat for doing his business so well on the walk.)

Brandy spun around briskly on her heels. She didn't bring the coffee cup with her but, instead, leaned against the counter and crossed her arms. "It's just that my homepage was open, and I have my computer set to sleep after ten minutes if it's not in use. I haven't been on the computer in an hour. There's no way my homepage would still be open."

I shrugged and mentally kicked myself for such a rookie mistake. In my defense, I hadn't expected her to notice or go right over to check her desk.

"Obviously, I wouldn't be able to log into your laptop. I don't know your password."

She glanced over at her dog. Fudgy was still staring up at her with a 'where's my treat' look. And it worked. Angry as she seemed to be, she wandered over to the dog cookie jar and pulled out a treat. That gave her an idea. I was also kicking myself for not realizing just how smart Brandy was.

"You're a dog mom," she said. "I'll bet your password has to do with your dogs' names."

I forced a smile. "Possibly. What about Sylvia's password?" I was going on offense now. Defense was making me feel inept and vulnerable. "I'll bet you knew all of her passwords. Even the one that allowed you to get into her phone so you could send Benny the fake text about floral wire." It seemed our donut and coffee chat was over. I stood up so as not to be trapped between her table and the wall in case things went drastically south. "You were the last person in the building. You locked Benny inside. You knew Sylvia was a micromanager, who liked to keep control of everything. You knew she'd drive the float herself if Benny couldn't be found."

Brandy's pink complexion drained of color, then it returned much darker. "You don't know what you're talking about. Here, I thought you wanted to be my friend. You're even worse than that monster, Sylvia. At least she had the decency to be straight out rotten to me."

"But she helped you with your mom and the house," I reminded her of the words I'd heard directly from her.

"That's because I discovered that she was blackmailing Arthur Andrews. I told her I'd let the police in on the plot if she didn't catch our house up on mortgage payments."

I nodded. "You were blackmailing the blackmailer."

"I was used to her treating me like garbage but then she went too far, humiliating me in front of everyone."

"When you asked to ride on the float," I said.

"That's right. You were there. You were there for all of it. Honestly, I didn't think it would work. I knew it was a long shot. I just wanted her to pass out, crash the float and be fired from the committee forever. She lived for that stupid parade where she could boss everyone around. I didn't think anything about her weak heart. So, you see, I didn't really kill her. Her bad heart killed her."

My best bet was to let her think exactly that. I was inside her house. I'd snooped around on her computer and probably wouldn't come out of this whole thing smelling like a rose. "You know what, you're right. If nothing else, it was all just a terrible accident." One that involved some planning, sealing shut the exhaust flap and even framing another person, but I'd let the police sort that out. "Your best bet is to go to the station and tell them everything you just told me, that you were just trying to teach Sylvia a lesson."

Brandy laughed. It was an evil sound. "Nice try. This is your word against mine. And I caught you snooping around my personal belongings."

"You invited me into your house." Then it dawned on me. "You knew when you asked me inside. You took the dog out because you knew I wasn't here for a friendly chat. You expected me to snoop around."

She shrugged casually. "You're a reporter. You can't help yourself." Her whole demeanor changed as if she had multiple personalities. "Now, take your donuts and your false pretenses and on your drive home, hope that I don't contact the police about the nosy reporter."

"Wow," I said. "I guess you were keeping this dark side of your personality hidden."

"Thank Sylvia for that. I learned from the best."

"I can't thank her." I picked up the box of donuts. "You killed her, remember?" I had to admit, on my way to the door, I was nervous that she might come up behind me with a knife or a heavy frying pan.

She must have sensed that I was worried she might attack me. Her new laugh really did sound like Sylvia's cold, dry cackle. "I wouldn't kill you. After all, I'm not in trouble. I didn't do anything except allow a ruthless reporter into my home. They'll send Arthur to jail for this, and that will be that."

I opened the door, stepped safely outside and turned with my box of donuts. "I think you're living in a fairy tale."

Her scowl sent a shiver down my spine. "Get off my property before I have you arrested," she snarled before slamming the door shut in my face.

I hurried off her property and to the jeep before she rethought the whole kill the nosy reporter idea. I pulled down the block, parked and called Jackson. He answered on one ring.

"Hey, Bluebird, I am so bored. What are you up to?"

"Some of us have to work... and solve murders. It was Brandy, the cheerful, sweet, subservient assistant. Only she's none of those things under that innocent exterior. She searched for information about carbon monoxide poisoning. I saw it in her search history when I was—" I stopped.

"When you were snooping around in her house," he finished for me.

"Yep. No sense in denying. By the way, there might be a complaint about me from said murderer."

"Sunni," he started.

"She invited me in. There were donuts and mentions of a friendly gal chat."

The microwave beeped in the background. "Hmm, my frozen enchiladas are ready. I don't think we can arrest someone for looking up carbon monoxide poisoning when half the town probably searched it once they heard what happened."

"I know that but she confessed to doing it."

I could literally hear him freeze in place. "She confessed?"

"Yep. Like I said, I left there with an entirely different opinion of Brandy than I had just an hour ago. No wonder she and Sylvia worked well together. They were both inherently rotten. And Brandy discovered that Sylvia was blackmailing Arthur Andrews, so she, in turn, blackmailed Sylvia. It was a whole blackmailing chain."

A second call beeped through on Jackson's phone. "Hold on, that's the precinct. I'll let them know what's going on." He switched to the other call and came back a few minutes later. "The lab was able to pick up a clear print on Sylvia's phone that didn't match the victim's. They can't find a match in the database."

"That will be Brandy's print. She's probably not in the database because up to this point she was a polite, kind person. Brandy knew Sylvia's passcode. She sent the text to Benny then locked him in the closet. That way Sylvia had to drive the float. Brandy insisted she only meant to humiliate Sylvia by causing her to pass out and ruin the parade. She claimed she didn't know Sylvia had health issues that would make her more susceptible to carbon monoxide poisoning."

"Sounds like you did a good job, Bluebird. I'm going to hang up so I can tell them to bring in Brandy. Maybe we should celebrate tonight with a dinner out."

"Aren't you eating enchiladas?" I asked.

"Those are just a pre-dinner appetizer."

"If we do start a farm, we're going to have to learn how to grow food so we can keep you fed. I'll see you tonight. I've got a story with a big scoop to write. That lead reporter job is as good as mine… again."

CHAPTER 35

*N*ow don't do anything—you know—anything ghost-
ish. No jumping out or saying boo or whatever might
frighten her." I paced the kitchen for the hundredth time.
Edward watched me swing from side to side of the kitchen with
arrogant indifference as if he was watching the world's most
boring tennis match.

"Once again, I've not said the word *boo* ever except to tell you
that I don't use the word boo. And now you've made me say it
twice. You're certain this is a good plan? You look as if you're one
step from the asylum with your incessant pacing, hand wringing
and babbling to yourself."

I stopped my pacing to look him straight in his transparent
blue eyes. "Thank you, as always it is good to have your support.
Raine deserves this. She saved Jackson's life. I have no way to
repay her, but this will be a nice little down payment."

"If you think that saving his life is worth repayment you
might consider a nice teapot set or a basket of fruit."

I gave him a proper eye roll and restarted my march across
the kitchen. "Maybe I made too many big decisions this week.

The whole not starting the inn and staying a journalist thing and—"

"And there was that rather questionable dress you chose to wear out of the house."

I swung back to look at him.

He stared back at me in confusion. "Oh, was that not part of the big decisions of the week. I thought surely you must have regretted that one. My mistake. Carry on with the trot."

"You're so helpful. We'll just start to call you that, Mr. Helpful." I stopped in front of him again. "Is it a mistake?" I asked. The front door opened. "Good, Jackson is here. I'll ask him because you are only making me more anxious." I hurried to the hallway and nearly ran into Jackson. I threw my arms around him. "I need a hug."

"Happy to oblige." We stood in each other's arms for a long, bracing moment.

"Am I making a mistake? I just think this would be so important to Raine. She'll, no doubt, be angry at me for keeping it secret for so long." We headed into the kitchen. "That might be why I'm so nervous about this. What if she gets mad that I've kept it from her and she walks out and we never talk again?"

Jackson kissed my nose. "I think you're overthinking this. Raine will be so blown away, she won't have time to wonder why you didn't tell her before. That said, if you decide not to do this, I'm with you on that too."

"Argh, that's almost as helpful as Edward."

"All I'm saying is this is your decision to make, and I support you both ways."

"I'll take all the support I can get. I need to get my mind off this. How was your first day back? What happened with the Sylvia Franco case?"

"The print on Sylvia's phone belonged to Brandy. It wasn't enough evidence, but after some good interrogation and negotia-

tion with the lawyer she hired, we got her to sign a full confession. She had been subjected to years of abuse from the victim so
that will help her side of the case, but she'll be doing time."

"And her dog?"

"Fudgy-poo has gone to live with Brandy's neighbor."

"That's good. I almost didn't want to turn her in because I
worried little Poo would get sent to a shelter."

Jackson chuckled as he walked to the refrigerator. "That does
not surprise me. How are we doing this big reveal?"

"Now you've revived the topic, but I suppose I can't avoid it
altogether. Raine will be here any moment. She thinks she's
coming for blueberry muffins and coffee." As I said it, Jackson
picked up one of the muffins I'd baked and shoved it in his
mouth. "If there are any muffins to offer by the time she gets
here."

"I promise I'll just eat this one. Besides, something tells me
Raine won't be thinking about blueberry muffins once you intro-
duce her to Mr. Annoying."

"Said like a true gentlemen with crumbs literally falling out of
his mouth," Edward drawled. "Were you raised in an actual
barn? Or maybe it was a cave."

"No, no, no, no, none of this between you guys. Not this
morning. I need full tranquility." A knock sounded on the door
and I shrieked. "It's her! It's Raine!"

"Our views on tranquility are entirely different." Edward
vanished.

"Where are you going? Remember, no big scary, sudden
entrances. And wait until I summon you." I flinched. "Sorry, not
summon, call." I looked at Jackson. "He hates that word. Insists
it's only for servants."

"Glad his snobbishness isn't rubbing off on you," Jackson
teased.

I waved off his commentary and smoothed my shirt and hair. "How do I look?"

Jackson nearly choked on a muffin crumb. "Are you expecting a date?"

I waved at him again. "So much support. Don't know what I'll do with all this extraordinary support," I muttered as I walked down the hallway. I took a deep breath and opened the door.

Raine pushed right past me without a hello. "Just dealt with the grumpiest old man at the hardware store. I needed a box of nails because my stupid, ancient old house is falling apart at the seams, and he kept telling me I was buying the wrong size. Some of the crown molding is peeling off the ceiling." She continued straight to the kitchen and made a beeline for the muffins. She stopped talking long enough to bite a muffin. She held up the partially eaten muffin. "Hmm, these are good. From a box?"

I took a moment from my utter state of anxiousness to be slightly insulted. "I am capable of following a recipe."

"I know. Sorry. That was catty." She took another bite. "So good."

"All right. I confess. It was from a box. Anyhow, have a seat. There is something far more important I need to talk to you about than muffins." I glanced over at Jackson. He was giving me an 'are you sure' brow lift. I wasn't going to debate it any further either externally or internally.

I sat across from her. She'd finished her muffin and looked up at me. "What's up?" she asked in that clipped, fun way someone might ask over a casual phone call. Then, being Raine, she realized something was *really* up. "Uh oh, that's a stony expression." She glanced at Jackson, but he was doing the cowardly look everywhere but at Raine trick.

"First of all," my voice sounded a little raw, like I'd been screaming and singing at a rock concert all night. I cleared my throat.

I wasn't going to tell her something this big sounding like a frog. "First of all, as you know, Jackson and I are so grateful to you. You saved his life. There's no other way to look at it. We both owe you so much. We're so thankful for your obvious gift, your incredible sixth sense."

Raine didn't blush easily but a red flush covered her cheeks and even crept up to her forehead. "I'm just glad I was there to help."

"We are too," Jackson said, finally emerging from his cone of silence. He sat down next to me, but I sensed that was as involved as he was going to get in what was about to take place. I'd put all seeds of doubt deep in the soil. I was going through with this. I owed it to Raine.

"So, here goes," I said and took another breath.

Raine's bracelets clinkered against the table as her hand shot across. She took hold of mine. "Oh wow, are you two getting married? I can't believe it!"

"Wait, what?" I looked at Jackson, who looked just as stunned as I felt. "No, sorry, if that's what you thought. No engagement. No, this is something much bigger."

Jackson cleared his throat to let me know he was a little insulted. I reached over and squeezed his arm. "Of course, that would be huge too, but this is bigger in a different way." I was losing control of the whole conversation. I'd practiced it a hundred times, in the bathroom mirror, the glass on the microwave, even on the side of the toaster, and now it was all slipping away. "Look, Raine," I said sternly enough to let everyone know I didn't want any more interruptions. "Since I moved here, we could say, without exaggeration, that you've been obsessed with the prospect of the Cider Ridge ghost."

She shrugged half-heartedly. "Not sure if obsessed is the right word."

"It's absolutely the right word," a posh English voice drifted around the kitchen. Edward had made himself heard, but he had not appeared. None of this was going as I'd planned.

Raine hopped up from her chair. The earlier pink blush had been completely erased. She glanced wildly around the room, then looked and pointed at Jackson. Her laugh sounded nervous, tense. "You almost had me, Jax. Nice job on the English accent."

Edward scoffed from somewhere in the kitchen. "Please, that barbarian couldn't speak proper English if he was reading straight from a Shakespearean play."

"I definitely can't if your idea of proper English is that wordy gibberish Shakespeare wrote," Jackson replied. It seemed the floodgates were open. Each syllable from Edward sent Raine a step back. I half expected her to run from the kitchen.

I got up and circled around to her side of the table. "What's going on, Sunni?" she asked nervously.

I took hold of both of her hands and looked her in the eyes. "That's what I'm trying to tell you. First of all, this has to stay secret. I know it'll be hard, but you can't talk about it to any of your psychic friends. The Cider Ridge Inn does have a ghost. Edward Beckett has been haunting the hallways of this house for nearly two centuries."

"Haunting, why always haunting." Edward's disembodied voice drifted around the kitchen.

Raine looked frantically around the room. "But—how—can I see him?"

Then, with all the flair and drama of a diva walking on stage, Edward made himself visible. He was standing right in front of the kitchen window so the light and the particles of dust could float through his image.

Raine's hands squeezed mine. I sensed she was holding her breath. Suddenly, the pressure on my hands disappeared and my best friend, the woman who held séances for the sole purpose of talking to ghosts, slipped to the floor in a dead faint.

Jackson's chair scraped the ground as he rushed over to help me. I was holding Raine's head in my lap. Jackson hurried over to the sink to wet a dishtowel.

"Certainly didn't expect this," Edward said. "And from a ghost expert, no less."

"Your sarcasm is not needed right now." I reached for the wet cloth and pressed it against Raine's forehead. She came to almost immediately, but she was confused and disoriented.

She turned her head to look up at me. "What happened? Why am I on the ground?"

"You fainted." I pressed the cloth against each cheek.

With some effort she sat up. "I don't understand."

"What's the last thing you remember?" Jackson asked.

Raine rubbed the side of her head. I'd caught her in plenty of time to make certain she didn't hit it.

"We were all talking about..." She looked at me. "We were talking about ghosts." Her voice got thin and raspy. "And then—" It was all coming back to her. She reached for my hand. "He's real then. Edward Beckett is in this house?"

I looked around the room. Edward had vanished, insulted by her reaction. He took his ghostliness and people's reactions very seriously. "Edward," I called out. "Please make yourself visible."

Edward's image rolled slowly into view. Raine stared up at him. She was still holding my hand, tightly. After a few long moments, the color returned to her face. She looked at me. "He's very handsome."

"Huh, maybe I misjudged her," Edward drawled. "She seems quite astute."

I sighed. "You'll soon discover that he's not just handsome but extremely—"

"Annoying," Jackson supplied a word. Not exactly the one I was thinking of but it worked.

"You can't tell anyone, Raine. Please," I added in for good measure.

Raine was still shaken, but she was coming around. "Don't worry. Your tall, handsome secret is safe with me." Her gaze drifted up and down. "I love his outfit."

Edward scoffed. "Did she just call my wardrobe an outfit? I'll have you know one of the finest tailors in London made this waistcoat."

Jackson looked at Raine. "Do you see what I mean?"

CHAPTER 36

*J*ackson and I sat out on the front stoop to watch the fireflies twinkle in the tall grasses across the road. I rested my head against his shoulder. "What a beautiful night. Perfect after a long, eventful week."

"That's right." Jackson picked up his glass of iced tea. "With all that's happened, we forgot to celebrate your promotion to lead reporter."

I picked up my glass, and we toasted my new position. "Can't believe I had to prove myself twice to get lead reporter on a tiny local newspaper. My college professors wouldn't exactly be crowing with pride. But I'm happy. And I'm happy about my decision not to open the inn. At least not yet."

"I'm happy if you're happy," Jackson said.

I laughed and lifted my head to look at him. "Is that like your 'I support you no matter what you decide' line? You sure like to take the easy way out."

"You're right. I'm glad you're not opening the inn, and it's mostly for selfish reasons. I want to be able to spend more time with you. There—direct enough?"

"That's better." I put my head on his shoulder again. "I did not expect Raine to faint. She told me her blood pressure runs low, and she has fainted on several occasions. She also said she was mortified that she fainted at the first sight of a real ghost. She swore me to secrecy on the matter. It looks like we each have a major secret to keep."

"That works. It's like someone blackmailing a blackmailer. Good job on the case, by the way."

"Thank you. I was rather pleased with myself too."

Our chat fell silent as we watched the fireflies with their glowing behinds dance in the darkness.

"I'm so glad I moved into this house," I said.

"Me too, Bluebird. Me too."

ABOUT THE AUTHOR

London Lovett is the author of the Firefly Junction, Port Danby, Frostfall Island and Starfire Cozy Mystery series. She loves getting caught up in a good mystery and baking delicious new treats!

Subscribe to London's newsletter [londonlovett.com] to never miss an update.

You can also join London for fun discussions, giveaways and more in her **Secret Sleuths** Facebook group.

https://www.facebook.com/groups/londonlovettssecretsleuths/

Instagram @LondonLovettWrites
Facebook.com/LondonLovettWrites

Find all available books at LondonLovett.com